The MAGICIAN'S BIRD

·A TUCKERNUCK MYSTERY·

The
MAGI

Illustrated by

ANTONIO JAVIER CAPARO

EMILY FAIRLIE

CIAN'S BIRD

·A TUCKERNUCK MYSTERY·

KATHERINE TEGEN BOOKS
An Imprint of HarperCollins Publishers

Katherine Tegen Books is an imprint of HarperCollins Publishers.

The Magician's Bird: A Tuckernuck Mystery
Text copyright © 2013 by Emily Ecton
Illustrations copyright © 2013 by Antonio Javier Caparo

Library of Congress Cataloging-in-Publication Data
Fairlie, Emily.
    The magician's bird : a Tuckernuck mystery / Emily Fairlie ; Illustrated
by Antonio Javier Caparo. — First edition.
        pages   cm
    Summary: "While planning a scavenger hunt for their classmates,
rising seventh graders Laurie, Bud, and Misti attempt to prove that their
beloved school founder is innocent in the murder case of Marchetti the
Magician"— Provided by publisher.
    ISBN 978-0-06-211893-6 (hardcover bdg.)
    [1. Treasure hunt (Game)—Fiction. 2. Schools—Fiction. 3.
Historic buildings—Fiction. 4. Mystery and detective stories.] I.
Caparo, Antonio Javier, illustrator.   II. Title.
PZ7.F1665Mag 2013   2012051738
[Fic]—dc23   CIP
                                                                  AC

Typography by Erin Fitzsimmons
13 14 15 16 17 CG/RRDH 10 9 8 7 6 5 4 3 2 1

First Edition

To Desmond,
the newest Fairlie

PART ONE

KEEP BEHIND THE LINE

Laurie flattened herself against the wall and wished she was invisible. She didn't think she'd been spotted, but she couldn't be sure. That last dash across the hall had been pretty risky.

Laurie took a deep breath and let it out slowly. If she breathed really shallowly, they probably wouldn't hear her. Of course, if she breathed too shallowly, she would pass out, which would kind of defeat the purpose. It's hard not to notice an unconscious kid sprawled out on the floor.

Of course, it didn't really matter how she breathed with Bud Wallace right next to her, panting like a winded water buffalo. Bud Wallace obviously didn't know anything about breath control.

"Shut up, Bud," Laurie hissed. "They'll hear you!"

Bud nodded and panted slightly less loudly, making him sound more like a wheezy donkey or an asthmatic Shetland pony. Laurie was too preoccupied to decide which.

The footsteps were coming closer.

"Now follow me, and I'll show you how it all began."

Laurie pressed herself closer to the wall. There was no going back now. They were here. It was the tour.

Flyer taped to every telephone pole on Main Street and tucked under the windshield wiper of every car at the strip mall

TUTWEILER TOURS!

Tour TUCKERNUCK HALL, ancestral home of MARIA TUTWEILER and the spirited TUCKERNUCK CLUCKERS, and the site of her world-famous treasure hunt!

SEE long-lost works of art by Pablo Picasso! Alexander Calder! Henry Moore! James Earle Fraser!

FOLLOW the mysterious clues laid out by legendary town celebrity MARIA TUTWEILER!

HEAR never-before-known information about the harrowing treasure hunt!

BE A PART OF HISTORY!

Tours given by local history expert Candy Winkle, wife of Tuckernuck Hall's own Princi"PAL" Martin Winkle.

Discounts for groups of ten or more; tours given twice daily and on appointment.

Call for reservations/information.

Great for Birthdays! Anniversaries! Visiting Grandchildren!

"Now if you'll turn your attention to the small gap in the frame here, you'll see where Maria Tutweiler cleverly hid the first clue. Mind the ropes, now, don't get too close. And remember, our number one rule here at Tuckernuck Hall is *no touching*!"

Laurie rolled her eyes at Bud. No touching, what a laugh. When she and Bud had been trying to find the treasure at the beginning of the year, half of the clues had spent time in the bottom of her gym bag. Bud had even stuck one of them down the back of his pants. But now that the treasure was the salvation of Tuckernuck Hall, everything was off-limits—the clues, the treasure, everything. It seemed like half of the school was behind velvet ropes now. On the last day of school, Misti Pinkerton had accidentally bumped into the bust of Homer in the English hall while retrieving a dropped pencil—and sent the whole school into lockdown. Complete with alarms, flashing lights, the whole shebang. It was pretty embarrassing.

Ever since the word "treasure" had appeared in the paper, gawkers had started hanging around the school to see what the fuss was about. And it didn't take long for Principal Winkle and his wife, Candy, to smell a moneymaker. And apparently moneymakers had to be protected at all costs.

It hadn't been that bad when school was going on, since creepy adults weren't generally allowed to lurk on school grounds. But ever since summer break had started, creepy lurking had been encouraged, and since Laurie and Bud were supposed to be at school planning the new scavenger hunt, they'd been spending more and more time crouching in doorways, hiding behind desks, and generally trying to become invisible.

It wasn't working.

Laurie could hear Candy Winkle's piercing voice just around the corner. She cringed. Laurie hadn't even known Principal Winkle was married until Candy showed up to start giving tours. It was true what they said—sometimes ignorance really was bliss.

"Now, the *amazing* thing about the discovery is that at this school, with a faculty and staff of intellectuals and scholars . . ."

Bud stifled a snort. Laurie glared at him, but she couldn't blame him. That part about intellectuals and scholars was pretty funny.

". . . it was a couple of sixth graders who found the first clue. *Sixth* graders. Isn't that the absolute end?" Candy gave a trilling laugh that made Laurie want to punch her in the face. "Personally, I'm amazed the clues actually got solved, and didn't just end up in the bottom of a locker somewhere!" She laughed like it was the world's funniest joke, which maybe it was to Candy Winkle.

The tour group laughed too. Laurie clenched her fists. Bud shook his head. "They're not worth it," he whispered. Not that Laurie would really punch Candy Winkle. At least he didn't think she would. She was all talk.

"And as you may have heard," Candy continued, "those sixth graders are responsible for putting together a new scavenger hunt for next year's students. Sixth graders! So you know what that means! You'd all better study up on your gummi-bear and video-game trivia!" She laughed again.

Bud suddenly understood the clenched fist response. "What is she even talking about? Does she understand how this scavenger hunt works *at all*?" Bud said. Like they'd seriously include a clue about gummi bears. Gummi bears weren't even a topic of conversation, as far as he was concerned.

"Rising seventh graders," Laurie said under her breath, huffing angrily. "We're not *sixth graders*. We're rising seventh graders," she said, smacking her fist into her palm.

Unfortunately, it was a loud smack.

Laurie looked down at her hand in horror, and then up at Bud, who was shaking his head.

"Way to go, Bruiser," he said under his breath. Then he jerked his head in the direction of the tour group sounds.

A pudgy man in an I HEART MARIA TUTWEILER shirt and a shapeless hat was leaning around the corner, staring at them like he'd just discovered a couple of rare and exotic animals.

Laurie groaned. Busted.

What to Do When You've Been Busted by a Creepy Tour Member
by Laurie Madison, rising seventh grader

1. Smile widely and blink your eyes. It buys you time and makes you look cute, like a baby bunny.
2. Identify all escape routes.
3. Feign emergency situation—appendicitis, extreme need to pee, projectile vomiting, that sort of thing.

4. MOST IMPORTANTLY: AVOID CANDY WINKLE
   AT ALL COSTS. AVOID EYE CONTACT. DO NOT
   ENGAGE.

"Is that who I think it is?" High heels clicked across the floor.

Bud smacked Laurie on the arm. "Way to go."

Laurie's eyes got wide. Escape plan number three, activate. "Quick! Bathroom! I have to—"

"It is!" Candy Winkle appeared around the corner and stopped, putting her hand on her hip and shaking a finger at Bud and Laurie.

Laurie wilted against the wall. Plan number three would do no good now that Candy Winkle had them in her clutches.

In the beginning, Laurie and Bud had made the mistake of thinking that the tour groups were pretty much like squirrels—cute and basically harmless. That was before Laurie had caught some tour woman trying to cut off a piece of her hair as a souvenir, and some guy had stolen half of Bud's sandwich to sell on eBay.

It was just weird. The kids at school had gotten over the whole Tuckernuck treasure thing after a couple of weeks. And it wasn't like Bud and Laurie were actual celebrities. But try telling that to Candy's tour groups. They were crazy for anything Tuckernuck, and Candy wasn't helping matters.

Candy smirked at them. "Now, you two don't have to hide. Gather round, everyone," she called over her shoulder to the slow-moving group of tourists. "We've got a couple of celebrities for you to meet!" The tour group jostled forward to get a better look at Bud and Laurie. They didn't look like they were one hundred percent convinced that they were looking at celebrities, but their cameras flashed anyway. Laurie rolled her eyes and was caught midflash. She was going to look awesome in somebody's photo album.

"Now this is Buck and Loni, they're the sixth graders I was telling you about. Isn't that right, kids? You found the treasure?"

The tour pressed closer. Laurie could almost feel their breath.

Bud shifted uncomfortably. "Uh. Right. That was us. Buck and Loni." He gave Laurie a sideways glance. Laurie bit her lip hard. She was not going to crack up in front of Candy Winkle.

"So are you here to plan the new scavenger hunt? Any secret hiding places you can reveal? Just between us?"

Another camera flash went off.

"Sure, I guess." Laurie said slowly, sizing up the crowd. If she ducked around the man with the floppy hat, she'd have a clear shot at the door. Bud would have to fend for himself. She couldn't save everybody. "I guess we could tell you . . ."

"That you're ten minutes late for your organizational scavenger hunt meeting? And that you've been keeping Miss Abernathy waiting while you play at being celebrities?"

Laurie felt Miss Abernathy's hand clamp down on her shoulder. She didn't think that was very fair. It wasn't like they'd planned on being late. But they could hardly be expected to just walk up to the office door while there was a tour group there. There was only so much they could take.

Miss Abernathy tightened her grip on Laurie's and Bud's shoulders as she pushed them past the crowds into her office. "Now. Let's get started."

List of Hiding Places for Scavenger Hunt
by Laurie Madison and Bud Wallace,
rising seventh graders

1. Buried in backyard (complete with treasure

map and accessible by treasure mark, X marking spot).

2. Underneath a floorboard in cafeteria.
3. Hidden in chandelier outside Reynolds Auditorium.
4. In dumbwaiter in cafeteria kitchen.
5. Hidden behind the dancing frog painting in school entryway (second choice, bowl of fruit).
6. In the window seat in the library.
7. In the catwalks of the auditorium. (Bud Wallace does not endorse this suggestion. Too dangerous.)
8. Hidden inside piano, attached to C flat wire.
9. Underneath the globe in the library.
10. Hidden in the deluxe gerbil habitat, in Ponch and Jon's food dish. (Laurie Madison does not endorse this suggestion. Too dangerous.)

Tools needed: Shovel, jigsaw, ladder, matte knife, crowbar, hammer, nails, chisel, parchment, quill and ink, etc.

Miss Abernathy looked at their list for a long time, then put it down on the desk in front of her with a pinched expression on her face. She took a pencil out of her pencil cup, sharpened it, and then held it poised over the paper while she looked at them for a long second.

"These are your suggestions?" she said finally, pressing her lips together tightly. She didn't look pleased with them. Laurie and Bud hadn't really been on her favorite student list ever since she caught them "attempting to destroy school property," as she put it. (Finding the treasure, as everyone else put it.)

"Well, yeah," Bud said. He thought that was pretty obvious. The name of the list pretty much explained that. Not a lot of ambiguity there. Bud wondered what kind of background you had to have to get a job as a school administrator.

"We have other ideas that we didn't put down, though," Laurie said, glancing at Bud. She didn't like the expression on Miss Abernathy's face at all. Sure, some of their ideas were a little elaborate. But that's just because the Laurie-and-Bud Scavenger Hunt was going to be so awesome. "We're willing to be flexible. Like the singing cherubs in the music hall? We could do something with them. Or with the founding fathers in the history wing. We didn't want to put too much stuff down at first, though."

Miss Abernathy gave a tight smile, "Yes. I see. Well." She made a few notations on the paper and then pushed the list forward on the desk. "You must realize these are all completely unrealistic."

"What? Why?" Laurie and Bud said over each other.

"Digging in the school yard? Prying up floorboards? Damaging a musical instrument? Absolutely not. You can't have seriously thought we'd allow that." She opened a folder on her desk and took out two pieces of paper. "I was afraid something like this might happen, so I came up with a few ideas of my own. I suggest you take a look and we can discuss them at our next organizational meeting. I think you'll find these ideas to be much more realistic."

"So our ideas are definitely out?" Laurie said slowly. "We can't do them?"

"That's right." Miss Abernathy pushed the copies of her list toward them.

"All of them. Definitely out," Bud echoed.

"Yes."

"So no digging," Laurie said. She wanted to be absolutely clear on that point.

"No digging."

Laurie and Bud exchanged a glance.

Miss Abernathy ignored it and pushed the papers forward again. "When we meet again this time tomorrow, I hope you'll have a more acceptable plan. Now, if you'll excuse me." Betty Abernathy stood up and waited. Technically, Maria Tutweiler's instructions left the scavenger hunt in Bud's and Laurie's hands, but that didn't mean Betty Abernathy had to accept it. She had ways of working around Tutweiler's eccentricities.

"Right," Laurie said blankly, before abruptly standing up and hurrying out. Bud hesitated only long enough to grab the papers off the desk before taking off after her.

Text message from Laurie Madison to Misti Pinkerton

MISTI! Abort plan! Stop! Will explain soon!

EMAIL
FROM: BETTY ABERNATHY
TO: PRINCIPAL MARTIN WINKLE
SUBJECT: TERRIBLE, TERRIBLE IDEA
Martin,

Let me say one more time how horrible this
idea of a scavenger hunt is. Do you realize these
children were planning to pull up floorboards
and climb in chandeliers? Surely this is not what
Maria Tutweiler intended.
Yours,
Betty Abernathy
P.S. I thought Olivia Hutchins was going to be
handling this with me? I can't take a whole
summer of those children alone.

~

"Tell me she isn't digging yet," Bud said as they skittered down the front steps and ran toward the side of the school. "We're going to totally get it if she's digging."

That morning it had seemed like a really good idea to have Misti Pinkerton look for a few prime digging spots for them.

She hadn't found the treasure with them, so she wasn't an official organizer of the scavenger hunt or anything. But they definitely couldn't have found it without her, and she had a bunch of good ideas for hiding places.

They'd figured having her scope out digging sites showed that they were being proactive. Taking initiative. Not a sign that they were ensuring their own doom.

"She said she was just going to do some surveying." Laurie said, her sneakers slipping on the grass. Of course Misti Pinkerton had never been known for her self-restraint. Especially when she was armed with a shovel. And no matter how you cut it, Betty Abernathy wasn't going to be happy having a huge crater in the side yard. They hadn't come across any mounds of dirt or gaping holes so far, though, so that was definitely a good sign.

"There—up ahead," Bud gasped. "Misti, stop!"

Misti Pinkerton was standing next to the garden shed, looking thoughtfully at the floor inside. She jumped as Bud stumbled up against the shed wall next to her.

"Holy cow, guys, what's the big rush? Did Abernathy go for the plan? I've got the perfect place all worked out."

"Didn't you get my text?" Laurie panted.

"No digging. Did you dig yet? Stop," Bud gasped, turning around and sliding down the shed wall to a sitting position.

"What? No. Text?" Misti fumbled in the pocket of her shorts and pulled out her cell phone. It was hot pink plastic, with nice big buttons for pudgy, uncoordinated fingers. A little-kid phone. She shook it in Laurie's face. "Laurie, does this look like it can text?"

Laurie winced. "Sorry about that."

"My stupid phone has four buttons with pictures on them, Laurie. Pictures. That's the kind of phone my parents got me." Misti brandished her phone again menacingly before deflating with a huge sigh and shoving it in her pocket. "So, no, I didn't get your text. She said no digging?"

Bud snorted. "No digging. No anything. Nothing cool, anyway." He handed Misti the crossed-out list with Miss Abernathy's notes.

List of Hiding Places for Scavenger Hunt by Laurie Madison and Bud Wallace, rising seventh graders, as evaluated by Betty Abernathy

1. ~~Buried in backyard (complete with treasure map and accessible by treasure mark, X marking spot.)~~ *Digging absolutely prohibited.*
2. ~~Underneath a floorboard in cafeteria.~~ *No. Unthinkable.*
3. ~~Hidden in chandelier outside Reynolds Auditorium.~~ *No.*
4. ~~In dumbwaiter in cafeteria kitchen.~~ *No.*

5. ~~Hidden behind the dancing frog painting in school entryway (second choice, bowl of fruit).~~ *Absolutely not.*
6. ~~In the window seat in the library.~~ *No.*
7. ~~In the catwalks of the auditorium. (Bud Wallace does not endorse this suggestion. Too dangerous.)~~ *Completely unrealistic.*
8. ~~Hidden inside piano, attached to C flat wire.~~ *No.*
9. ~~Underneath the globe in the library.~~ *Allow students to manhandle a rare globe? I think not.*
10. ~~Hidden in the deluxe gerbil habitat, in Ponch and Jon's food dish. (Laurie Madison does not endorse this suggestion. Too dangerous.)~~ *Completely unacceptable and unhygienic.*

Tools needed: ~~Shovel, jigsaw, ladder, matte knife, crowbar, hammer, nails, chisel, parchment, quill~~ and ink, etc.

Ink approved, if contained in a leakproof ballpoint pen.

Misti grimaced. "At least she's letting you use ink.

That's . . . something."

Bud rolled his eyes. "Yeah, in pens, real big of her. She has her own ideas."

Misti poked her shovel at the wall and shook her head. "Maybe her ideas are good?"

Laurie folded her arms. "Yeah, right. I seriously doubt that."

Bud flattened the papers that he'd been clutching in his hands. "Fine, we'll at least give her a chance. There could be something here. She can't be totally lame, right?"

Laurie and Misti exchanged a glance. Then Laurie shrugged. "Okay. Let's see what she's got."

Suggestions for Appropriate
Scavenger Hunt Hiding Places
by Betty Abernathy, scavenger hunt
co-supervisor
(Olivia Hutchins, co-supervisor, in absentia)

1. Hidden in a fake rock in front of the school.
2. Under the doormat on the front porch.
3. Above a door frame to a classroom.

4. Pinned to the school activities bulletin board.
5. Hidden in an empty mail cubby.
6. Written on a blackboard.
7. Left with a friendly teacher or administrator. (This suggestion is ideal, because it could be used multiple times!)
8. On a windowsill INSIDE a room (perhaps behind a curtain for additional concealment).
Enjoy yourselves, kids!
Betty Abernathy

"Wow. You're right. These are worse than lame." Bud stared at the paper in shock.

"Pinned to the *BULLETIN BOARD*?" Laurie gaped at Bud. "Hidden in a FAKE ROCK? Please tell me you were kidding about the fake rock."

Bud shook his head. "It says right here, number one, fake rock."

"We can't hide a clue in a freaking fake rock! We'll be laughed out of school!" Laurie could hear the mocking laughter now. That was all she needed, to be the weirdo who hid a clue in a fake rock.

"Maybe she's flexible about the fake rock," Misti said.

"Maybe she'd go for one of those fake cans of deodorant or soup instead? Those can look pretty real."

"Look on the bright side," Bud said, folding the paper. "They won't laugh at us about the fake rock, because they'll be too busy laughing their butts off about the clue written on the blackboard."

Misti leaned against the shovel thoughtfully. "You know, if you just write clues on a blackboard, it would be really easy for someone to change. It could mess up the whole scavenger hunt."

Laurie shot her a dirty look. "We're not seriously considering the blackboard idea, Misti. Okay? Get real."

Misti looked offended. "Well, I was just saying. It's a bad idea." She stabbed the shovel in the dirt. "I'm AGREEING WITH YOU, OKAY?"

"Watch the shovel, Misti." Bud didn't think the stabbed place in the dirt could be tied to them, but he wasn't taking any chances.

"Sorry, Misti," Laurie said, kicking the ground to rough up the area around the stab mark. "It's just . . . Maria Tutweiler never would have made us write a clue on a stupid blackboard. She would've let us do something cool. I mean, a lame scavenger hunt is worse than no scavenger hunt at all!" Laurie blew a piece of hair out of her face. "So what do we do?"

Bud shrugged. "Well, we should probably—"

"Shhh, Bud. Company." Laurie nudged Bud with her foot and jerked her head toward the school. Candy Winkle and her group were coming around the corner.

"Seriously?" Bud said, smacking the ground. "Good grief, isn't anyplace around here private? This stinks!"

"Shovel, Misti," Laurie said under her breath.

"Right." Misti chucked the shovel into the shed just as Candy Winkle turned around and noticed them.

"Buck! Loni!" Candy waved at them. "And your little friend. Minty, isn't it?" She waved at Misti.

"Wave, Minty," Laurie said under her breath.

Misti shot her a nasty look and then plastered on a huge fake smile and waved merrily at the tour group.

"Good grief, they're still here? How long does this tour last?" Bud whispered, struggling to his feet and waving too. He still hadn't gotten over the whole sandwich-on-eBay thing. The seller had even hinted that some of Bud's spit was on the crust and could be used to clone a whole new Bud. It was hard to forget that kind of thing.

"Just smile and wave, Buck." Laurie waved heartily. She hadn't expected the grubby shed to be one of the attractions, but nothing Candy did surprised her anymore.

> ### How to Fool Tour Groups Into Thinking You're a Happy Camper When You'd Really Rather See Them Sink Into the Ground and Get Eaten by Slugs
> #### by Laurie Madison, rising seventh grader
>
> 1. Smile. (Again. The smile really is a cure-all when it comes to tour groups.)
> 2. Wave. (That makes them focus on your hand, and not the shovel your friend just chucked into the shed.)
> 3. Imagine them being devoured by slugs. This will make your smile bigger. (Or large slavering rats or rabid venomous squirrels, if slugs aren't your thing.)

"Keep smiling," Laurie said through clenched teeth.

The tour group oozed its way around Candy Winkle and toward the shed. The man with the floppy hat and Maria Tutweiler shirt was in the lead.

Candy was starting to look uncomfortable. That oozing wasn't a good sign. She'd lost control of the group.

"Thanks for saying hi, kids, but we're on a schedule. Gather round, everyone." She waved her arms ineffectually in an attempt to herd the group back into a manageable mass.

The man with the floppy hat ignored her and headed for Laurie. "Excuse me, but did she say you're one of the kids? That solved the puzzle?"

His voice was so soft that Laurie almost couldn't hear him. She nodded hesitantly. She hadn't expected the creepy guy to try to make actual contact.

"I was hoping you could help me. I . . ." He trailed off, glancing back at Candy Winkle.

Laurie leaned forward a little in spite of herself, to try to catch what he was saying. "Help you?"

"I was hoping . . . you see, it's about Maria Tutweiler—"

"Sir! Excuse me, sir." Candy Winkle tiptoed over, trying to keep her high heels from sinking into the yard. "Sir, please stay with the group. Leave the children alone, now. They're not a stop on the tour."

She grabbed the man firmly by the shoulder and pushed him in the direction of the rest of the group. "Sorry to bother you, kids. Wave bye-bye now!"

Laurie wasn't sure exactly who Candy expected to wave bye-bye, but if they were leaving, she was game. She elbowed Bud in the ribs and did the big smile and wave as the herd headed back around the corner and disappeared.

"Bye-bye!" Bud called.

"What did that guy want?" Misti sidled up to Laurie. "I like his shirt."

Laurie shrugged. "Beats me. Maybe he had a question about the scavenger hunt?" Laurie frowned. She was glad Candy had gotten rid of him, but still, she would've liked to know what the heck he was talking about.

"OH!" Misti gave a little jump. "I almost forgot! I found the perfect place!"

She hurried into the shed and picked up the shovel.

"Good grief, Misti, didn't you listen to anything we said? We can't dig!" Bud said, scowling.

"I know, okay? But check this out." She thumped the shovel against the wooden floor of the shed. "Hear that? Isn't that weird?"

Bud rolled his eyes. "It sounds like a floor."

"No, listen!" Misti thumped again. "This part over here isn't the same as the rest of the floor." She thumped on both sections to demonstrate. "See? It's kind of hollow sounding? Like, I don't know, different. And it feels weird, too, kind of springy or something. Less solid. See?" Misti bounced up and down and thumped again.

Laurie tried to hear the difference, but she just wasn't getting it. It was kind of irritating, to tell the truth. At least to Bud. He snapped.

"Misti, there is nothing weird about this floor, okay?" He stomped over and snatched the shovel out of her hands. "It's just a floor. See?" He did his own version of thumping, but he managed to make it sound sarcastic, somehow.

Laurie glanced back at the school. The tour group was gone, sure, but they couldn't be that far away. "Cut it out, Bud. We're not supposed to be busting on things. Someone could hear you."

"Hear me what, thump the floor? Or bounce on a springy floor?" Bud thumped again, really hard. It wasn't a kidding-around thump.

"You're going to get us in trouble." This was just the kind of thing Betty Abernathy would love to catch them doing. She was just itching to bust them for vandalism.

But Bud was on a roll. "See, Misti? Just a floor. No matter how many times you go thump. See? Thump thump thu—"

And Bud fell through the floor.

Misti and Laurie froze, staring at the Bud-shaped hole in horror.

It was like a cartoon—one minute he was there, the next he was gone.

"Hey, Misti? Laurie? Is that you?"

Laurie's head whipped around so fast she was surprised she didn't give herself whiplash. She groaned. This was not what she needed right now. She recognized that voice. It was Calliope Judkin.

How to Keep Your Archnemesis from Noticing That Your Friend Has Just Fallen Through a Hole in the Floor
by Laurie Madison, rising seventh grader

1. Friend? What friend?
2. Hole? What hole? I don't know what you're talking about.
3. What do you mean, why am I blocking the door? I'm not blocking anything. I'm just standing here.

Laurie did a quick mental review. Calliope Judkin was pretty much the biggest snoop there was and had spent a good part of the past year spying on them and leaking information to the newspaper and people trying to shut the school down. Not someone you'd turn to in a time of crisis.

She glanced back over her shoulder at the hole in the floor. Bud hadn't made a sound since he'd fallen though, which meant pretty much one thing. Bud was dead. Or unconscious with a broken leg. Either way, telling Calliope about it wasn't going to make him undead or un-unconscious with a broken leg. It would just guarantee that it was plastered all over the six o'clock news.

Laurie fought down her panic as Calliope bounced over. "Hey, guys, what's up?"

Misti and Laurie glanced at each other, eyes wide, and then casually positioned themselves in front of the door-way.

"Up? What are you talking about, nothing's up." Misti's voice was shrill enough that dogs in the next county winced at the sound.

Laurie tossed her hair in a calm and collected way. "Nothing's up, we're just standing here, okay? For no reason. But nothing's up. What makes you say some-thing's up?" Laurie cringed inside. That hadn't sounded nearly as calm and collected as she'd hoped. Of course, it's hard to sound calm and collected when you're standing in front of a hole with a dead body at the bottom. Not that she knew Bud was dead. But it was pretty likely, though, right? Way more likely than unconscious with a broken leg.

Calliope stared at them. "Oookay. Nothing's up. Good to know."

They stared awkwardly at one another for an uncomfortably long amount of time.

"Yeah, so what do you want?" Misti squeaked finally. Laurie glared at her. Way to be subtle, Misti.

Calliope looked disgusted. "Look, I was trying to be a friend, okay? I just thought you'd want to know about this." She smacked Laurie in the chest with a folded-up newspaper. "Check out the banner over the headline."

Laurie took the newspaper and unfolded it. It was a special afternoon edition of the *Morning News*, and the banner definitely wasn't good.

> # MARIA TUTWEILER'S CRIMINAL PAST!
> # EXCLUSIVE!!
> # TUTWEILER'S DIRTY SECRETS
> # REVEALED! ALL THIS WEEK

"What's this about?" Laurie said, staring at the paper. "Criminal past? What does that mean?"

Calliope shrugged. "Like I know. I wouldn't have even seen it if LeFranco hadn't handed it to me."

Walker LeFranco was the former school board president who'd been out to shut down Tuckernuck Hall, until Laurie and Bud had found the treasure and messed up his plans. Last Laurie'd heard, he had quit and had gone into the newspaper business.

"He's not trying to bring down the school anymore, is he? That's all over. He lost. We won." Laurie frowned and handed the newspaper back to Calliope.

"Yeah, well, not according to LeFranco. He's got plans. Big plans. And he's going to make sure this school gets shut down, one way or another."

"How do you know that?" Misti squeaked, glancing back over her shoulder at the hole.

"Because when he handed me the paper, he said, 'I've got plans. Big plans. And I'm going to make sure your school gets shut down, one way or another.' So that tipped me off." Calliope rolled her eyes. "Look, I'll let you get back to . . . doing nothing, okay? Just thought you should know."

"Yeah, well. Thanks," Laurie said. She knew she

should be more apologetic and grateful, but the whole hiding-the-corpse thing made it tough to be buddy buddy.

"Whatever," Calliope said, and stomped off across the lawn.

Misti and Laurie stared after her without moving as she rounded the corner.

> ## Note to Self
> ### by Calliope Judkin
>
> Laurie Madison and Misti Pinkerton are hiding something and acting in an EXTREMELY suspicious manner.
> (Is Laurie Madison EVER not doing something suspicious?) Investigate.

"He's dead, isn't he," Misti said without emotion.

"Probably," Laurie said. Bud hadn't made a sound since he'd fallen. Laurie took a deep breath and tried not to freak out.

She didn't even want to think about what she was going to say to Bud's dad. He'd really loosened up since they found the treasure—he'd stopped being all strict about studying for college and let Bud hang out a lot more. And where did it get him? With a kid who was dead or unconscious with a broken leg. Not good. Laurie braced herself for the worst and scrambled over to the hole. It wasn't going to be pretty.

"Bud?" she whispered loudly, peering down into the darkness. "Are you still alive?"

Bud's head poked up between the broken boards. "Oh, man, you guys!"

Misti squealed. "You're alive?"

"Yeah, I'm alive. And you're not going to believe this. I think I've found a secret room."

PART TWO

THE SECRET ROOM

The first thing Bud thought when he fell through the floor was, Wow, Misti was right after all. The second thing was, Man, that's going to bruise. Any other thoughts disappeared pretty fast as he looked around and realized where he was.

He'd expected to be under the floor of the shed, in a crawl space with rattraps, maybe. He didn't expect to be at the foot of a short stairway leading up to the shed floor. But that's just where he was. And in the gloom, he could see a narrow passageway leading off to his right. This wasn't some crawl space. This was something someone had built. This was a hallway.

Laurie's and Misti's voices drifted down through the hole. They were talking to someone up outside the shed, and it sure didn't seem like they were that concerned about what had happened to him. Well then, he didn't think they'd mind if he took the opportunity to do a little exploring on his own before he filled them in. Especially if he didn't tell them about it. It wasn't every day that he got to make a discovery all on his own. He was going to enjoy every minute of it.

Bud got to his feet and dusted off his butt. Then he dug around in his pocket until he found his penlight key chain and tested it out. Bud grinned. The battery still worked. Not many situations called for a tiny little flashlight, so he wasn't that sure it would work. (Actually, he could only think of one time he'd actually used it—in the community pool locker room that time Pete Simpkins thought something had died in the bathroom drain. The flashlight beam hadn't revealed any dead things, but that didn't mean they weren't there. Something sure had stunk.)

Bud shone the light into the darkness of the passageway and took a tentative step forward. The light didn't help much, but it was something.

The passage was much clearer than Bud thought an abandoned passageway would be—there wasn't any rubble or trash on the stone floor, and the walls seemed to be wood, not oozing, weepy concrete with gigantic spiders crawling on them. Which was definitely a plus.

The passageway turned up ahead, and instead of being cautious, Bud barreled around it and almost gave himself a concussion. Because right around the corner was a large wooden door.

Bud picked up his penlight from where he'd dropped it when he'd done a face plant into the wood and inspected the door. It was big. It was closed. And it looked creepy as all get-out. Although, to be honest, it could've been decorated with dancing bunnies holding balloons and barfing sparkly hearts, and it still would've been creepy.

He'd smacked into it pretty hard, and no one had opened the door, so that gave Bud a pretty good idea that there wasn't anyone on the other side. But there was only one way to be sure.

Bud shone the penlight on the crystal doorknob, took a deep breath, and reached down and grasped the knob. It turned in his hand. The door was unlocked. All he had to do was turn the knob completely and go inside.

Things to Consider Before Blindly Walking Through a Strange Door
by Bud Wallace, rising seventh grader
1. If the door is closed, it could be for a reason.
2. Maybe a really good reason, like rabid dogs inside, or venomous spiders.
3. Plus, a penlight isn't much light. Exploring strange rooms is better when you have a big flashlight or camping lantern.
4. Also, it really wouldn't be fair to explore without Laurie and Misti. They would be really upset. They'd probably cry.

5. Good guys don't make girls cry.
6. VERDICT: Probably best to put off
   exploring for the time being. Just to keep the
   peace with the ladies.

Bud hurried back around the corner and down the passageway just in time to hear Laurie's voice.

"Are you still alive?"

Bud clambered over the broken slats of wood and poked his head up through the hole. "You're not going to believe this. I think I've found a secret room."

Laurie didn't believe it. Most people fall through a floor and have traumas, injuries, gaping flesh wounds with lots of blood. Bud Wallace falls through a floor and finds a secret freaking room. It wasn't fair. But that didn't stop Laurie from launching herself through the hole and into the passageway, almost twisting her ankle on the low stairway in the process.

"Are those stairs? What is this place?"

Misti peered down at them through the hole. "I think this is actually a trapdoor. This piece here, next to the place Bud smashed, looks like a latch or something. . . ."

Misti fiddled with something on the underside of the floor and then pulled. The whole floor panel above Bud and Laurie swung open.

"Well, that's great, Misti, but fat lot of good it does now," Laurie said. "We've got the hole."

Misti nodded and tentatively crept down the stairs. "Yeah, for now. But unless I'm wrong, we're going to need to fix that hole so that no one notices it, right?"

Laurie caught her breath. She didn't even want to think about what Betty Abernathy would say if she saw it. "Right."

"And we'll still want to get down here, right? I mean, unless it's horrible, with deadly fungus and bloated corpses or something." Misti looked at Bud. "Did you see any?"

"Bloated corpses?" Bud looked pale. "Nope, not so far." He was really glad he hadn't thought of bloated corpses when he was making his mental list.

Misti picked up a piece of wood that had fallen with Bud. "I've got a hot glue gun at home. I bet we can make it look okay. We'll just need to make sure we don't forget and step on it."

"Yeah, okay," Laurie said. She wasn't one hundred percent sure that essentially booby trapping the floor of the shed was a great idea, but she wasn't going to argue now. Not when there were secret passageways to explore. "Where does that go, Bud?" She pointed down the passage. "Did you go down there?"

"Yeah." Bud grinned. "It goes to the door to the secret room."

Laurie's eyes gleamed. "That's awesome. What's inside?"

Bud shrugged. "Beats me, I don't know. I didn't look."

"You didn't look? How could you not look? It's a secret room!"

"I waited for you! Good grief, try to be a good guy . . . ," Bud muttered.

"That's really cool of you," Laurie said, smacking him lightly on the arm. She meant it, too. She didn't know if she would've been able to resist at least one peek inside. "Thanks, Bud."

Misti nodded. "That's probably where the bloated corpses are."

"Probably." Bud grinned. He would've grinned bigger if he'd been sure Misti was joking.

"Well, we'll see soon. Come on, let's go!" Laurie grabbed Bud's penlight and bounced down the passageway without a second glance.

Laurie was already at the door by the time Bud and Misti caught up to her. The penlight beam was bouncing up and down on the door as Laurie waited impatiently for them to catch up.

"This is it, right?" she said, still bouncing in frustration. Bud nodded.

"Then let's go!" Laurie reached out and turned the doorknob.

Things to Consider Before Blindly Walking Through a Strange Door
by Laurie Madison, rising seventh grader
1. How to split up the loot we find. Three ways?
2. Maybe gold items to Misti, diamonds and jewel-encrusted things to me, and other stuff to Bud.
3. Or maybe make decisions like that after we've seen the loot.

Things to Consider Before Blindly Walking Through a Strange Door
by Misti Pinkerton, rising seventh grader
1. Try not to step on the bloated corpses.

The door swung open, and Laurie, Bud, and Misti peered inside. It was kind of an anticlimax, though, since all they could really see was a tiny patch of red where the penlight was shining on something just inside the room.

"Well, this stinks," Laurie said finally. "What is that red thing? Can you see anything?" She took a few steps into the room and shone the flashlight around. "It looks like, what? Furniture or something?"

Bud followed her into the room and took a few steps past her into the blackness. "Ow!" he yelped. "What the heck is that?"

"What?" Laurie pointed the flashlight in the direction of Bud's legs, but all she saw was a blur of khaki as Bud jumped back. "What was it?"

"I don't know! Something was there!" Bud said, his voice about an octave higher than usual.

Laurie pulled out her cell phone and opened it, bathing her face in blue light. She leaned forward and handed Bud the penlight. "This is ridiculous. We can't see anything."

Bud took the penlight and immediately scanned the area around him. "We need to come back with a camping lantern or headlamp or something."

"Or we could try this," Misti's voice came from the door. And then suddenly the room was filled with light.

Bud and Laurie blinked from the sudden brightness. "How did you do that?" Laurie gasped.

"Light switch," Misti said, nodding her head in satisfaction. "Thought there must be one, and yep, there it was!"

"Light switch," Bud grumbled. He would've thought of that eventually. Probably he would've come up with it right off if Misti hadn't been going on and on about bloated corpses.

"Good grief, look at this place!" Laurie snapped her cell phone shut and looked around the room. She didn't know exactly what she'd been expecting—probably some kind of storage room or something. Filled with gold bars and jewels if she was lucky, old moldy boxes of files and junk if she wasn't. But she sure wasn't expecting this.

It was a room. And not just a room, but a really fancy room with Oriental-type rugs scattered on the floor and framed photos on antique wooden cabinets. The furniture was the old lady kind—tall wing chairs with hard velvet seats, a velvet couch with a wooden frame and claw-type arms, and lots of polished-looking wooden end tables and things. Laurie felt like she was on a stage set or in a museum or something.

It didn't look like a room that was abandoned. It looked like a room someone used. Or had used. Because everything in it looked about a hundred years old. It was like when they'd opened the door, they'd walked through a time warp.

"That what jumped you, Bud?" Laurie said. A plush red velvet footstool was next to Bud's leg. Laurie poked it with her toe.

"Look, it could've been anything, okay?" Bud muttered, nudging the footstool back at her with his foot. "What do you think this place is, anyway?"

"It's Maria Tutweiler's place." Misti looked up from a small rolltop desk on the other side of the room. She was examining a worn ledger book lying on top. "At least, all these things are hers. Her name's on this notebook. I'll bet it's her secret place."

"I'll bet you're right." Bud couldn't keep the goofy grin off his face. "A secret room. Man, how cool is that?"

Laurie peeked into a large cabinet next to the couch. It had a lattice-type front, and some kind of bird statue inside, and a bunch of ledgers like Misti was looking at lined up on a shelf below. "It's pretty cool, all right." She grinned back at Bud. She didn't see any jewels or gold bars or anything, but a secret room at school was pretty great. If she played her cards right, she'd never have to dress out for PE again.

"I can't believe no one knows about this!" Bud said, plopping down on the couch and putting his feet up on the inlaid coffee table. If nobody knew about the stuff in the room, Bud wasn't particularly worried about messing things up.

"But how can they not?" Laurie said, picking up a lion-shaped bookend and examining its feet. "Somebody knew once, at least. Did they just forget it was here?"

"Beats me. But they definitely don't know now. If they did, there would be teacher junk all over the place." Bud tried to scooch in to the couch and get comfortable, but it just really wasn't that kind of couch.

"Yeah, you're right." Laurie said, leaning against the chair. She looked at the plush rug and toed it with her sneaker. "Why would Maria Tutweiler have a secret room?" She couldn't help but think about the newspaper banner Calliope had showed her, and it gave her a weird feeling in the pit of her stomach. She didn't like the idea of Maria Tutweiler having secrets she didn't know about. And this room definitely proved that she did.

"Because it was cool? I don't know, do you need a reason?" Bud scoffed, settling against the stiff couch back. He made a mental note to try a chair next time. The couch was definitely not the place to sit.

"You're probably right." Laurie knew that if she had a secret room, she'd never come out, except maybe to sneak snacks out of the kitchen. It would be awesome.

She sighed. "I just wish we didn't have to tell Winkle about it."

"What? What do you mean?" Bud took his feet off the coffee table. Now that he'd thought about it, he didn't want to seem too comfortable. Not yet, anyway. Not until he'd had a chance to move some of his stuff in and really give it the ol' Bud touch. "Who says we're going to tell him?"

Laurie rolled her eyes. "Come on, Bud, you know we have to tell him. You think we can keep this secret?" She perched tentatively on the arm of the wing chair. She didn't want to mess anything up by touching it too much.

"I don't know, but don't you want to try?" Bud scooched down to the end of the couch. "Come on, Laurie, you know what's going to happen when we tell them. They'll cordon the whole place off with ropes, and we'll never get to see it again. Not up close. You'll never get to touch that stupid lion, and Misti will never be able to read that stupid notebook she's holding. Am I right? Misti, back me up here."

"It's in cursive, so I'm not really reading it anyway," Misti said, putting the ledger down. "I'm not really great at cursive," she admitted, sitting on the footstool. Laurie and Bud nodded sympathetically. Nobody liked cursive.

Misti shrugged. "But Bud's right. We can't even touch the spirit stick now, and you guys are the ones who found it."

Laurie made a face. The spirit stick was a sore subject. She and Bud had found the spirit stick at the beginning of the year, and according to the letter from Maria Tutweiler, they were in charge of it. But ever since they'd found it, it had been behind glass in the entryway to the school. Miss Abernathy had sent people to detention for breathing too close to the glass, that's how much she guarded it.

Laurie slid backward until she was sitting in the wing chair with her legs draped over the arm. She stroked the head of the lion bookend and sighed. Bud was right. They weren't allowed to do anything. But she knew Principal Winkle, too, and if he found out they'd been hiding something like this, their names would be dirt.

"Well, what if we just keep it secret for a little while? Maybe just a day or two?" Winkle would have to know eventually, sure, but it would be nice to have a secret hideout for a little while.

"That would work," Bud said, nodding happily. "I'm fine with a day or two. That would give us a chance to investigate a little more. Maybe see what everything is. Like that door over there, where does that go? We can't tell Winkle about this place without knowing stuff like that, right?"

Laurie hesitated. She did want to know where that door in the corner went, now that she'd noticed it. "Right, that makes sense."

Misti hopped up and ran to the strange small door. She opened it a crack and peered out.

"What is it?" Laurie held her breath. She really hoped the door didn't lead into Mr. Winkle's private office or the boys' bathroom or something. That would be bad.

"It's another passageway," Misti said. "It's just like the other one, except a little skinnier."

"Good grief, where could it go?" Laurie said, struggling to her feet. "Okay, Bud. Penlight. We've got to figure this out."

Bud got up and handed Laurie the penlight. "Sounds good to me."

Suddenly the room was filled with harsh electronic music.

"Oh, GOOD GRIEF!" Misti said, grabbing at her pocket.

"What the heck?" Bud said. "What is that?"

"'Samba Beat #5,'" Misti grumbled, pulling her neon-pink phone out of her pocket and pushing a button. "Hi, Mom, what's up?" She held a finger up at Bud and Laurie and rolled her eyes. "Yeah, I know what time it is. Yeah, I *know* I was supposed to be home. Fine. Okay. Fine. Bye." She pushed another button a little harder than it looked like she had to. "Well, guess what."

"You have to go," Laurie guessed.

"Yeah! She's all ticked off just because I'm a little late." Misti shoved the phone back in her pocket.

Bud got up. "Well, that settles it. We definitely don't tell anybody. And we come back tomorrow and explore that passageway. Deal?"

"Deal." Laurie said. "Tomorrow."

Laurie, Bud, and Misti peeked out of the shed, carefully scanning the yard for any signs of Calliope, tour groups, teachers, nosy squirrels, hidden cameras—anything at all that might pay too much attention to them. When the coast seemed to be clear, they hurried one by one across the lawn, trying to act as normal as possible. With varying degrees of success.

Candy Winkle watched Misti Pinkerton twirling and fist punching her way across the school driveway, and tapped her fingertip on her lips thoughtfully.

~

EMAIL
FROM: CANDY WINKLE
TO: PRINCIPAL MARTIN WINKLE
SUBJECT: Potential Tour Addict
Honey,
I was going through the sign-up sheet for tomorrow's tours, and that man is back again— the one that I told you about? He's come for the tour every day this week, and today he was even trying to talk to the kids. Do I need to cut him off? Is he addicted to our tours? I know my speech is fascinating, but I'm worried that he's a bit obsessed.
Kisses,
Candy

P.S. The kids are a bit . . . unusual, aren't they?

EMAIL
FROM: PRINCIPAL MARTIN WINKLE
TO: CANDY WINKLE
SUBJECT: Keep an Eye on Him
Snookie Bear,
I don't like him talking to the kids. If he goes
near them again, then yes, we'll take steps. But
otherwise, I don't think we need to worry just
yet. As long as he's paying and not bothering
anyone, I don't think there's any harm in it. (And
don't forget how many times I took the library
tour in college when you were working there!)
I'll bring it up with Police Chief Burkiss too, just
to see what he says.
See you tonight!
Your Lambikins
P.S. Yes, unusual is an understatement.

⚡

"So, did you see the thing in the paper? About Maria
Tutweiler?" Laurie said as she blopped salad dressing
onto her salad.

"I saw it," Laurie's mom said, frowning at Laurie's

bowl. "You know, you don't have to drown the poor let-
tuce. It's already dead."

Laurie made a face and handed the dressing to her
brother, Jack. "And?"

"And what?" Laurie's mom scooped out some noodle
casserole. "And I didn't give it much thought."

"Aren't you worried, though? He says she was a
criminal! With secrets!" Laurie didn't know what kind
of secrets Walker LeFranco was talking about, but
whatever they were, she knew they couldn't be good.
He could even know about the secret room, and she sure
didn't want that in the paper.

Laurie's dad smiled at her and handed her the basket
of rolls. "Laurie, think of Walker LeFranco as a little
dog. He may spend a lot of time yapping at your ankles,
but if you ignore him, he'll go away."

Laurie took the rolls doubtfully. She knew about little
dogs. Sometimes they could bite like nobody's business.

"So, Jack," Laurie's father said. "How's the odd-job
business going? Any new clients?"

Jack nodded and took the basket of rolls from Laurie.
"Mrs. Tysinger's having me mow her lawn once a week.
And I'm fixing the gutters on the old Hopkins place."

"That's great!" Laurie's dad grinned at Jack and took

a mouthful of casserole.

Laurie didn't want to talk about Jack's handyman jobs or some stupid gross gutters. She wasn't done with the LeFranco conversation yet. "So you think he's just yapping? LeFranco?"

Laurie's dad nodded at her. "He's just a lot of talk. Don't you think if he had anything on Maria Tutweiler, he would've used it by now? He's probably planning an exposé on how she forgot to water her plants."

Jack snorted. "Yeah, or maybe she didn't recycle. Or she wore white after Labor Day."

Laurie rolled her eyes. "Like they even had recycling back then."

"Don't worry, Laurie," Jack said, patting her hand. "Your precious Maria Tutweiler will survive whatever LeFranco comes up with, even if it is something as terrible as staying up too late."

Laurie bit off a hunk of roll and made a face at Jack. She wished she felt as confident as they did.

EMAIL
FROM: MRS. PINKERTON
TO: LAURIE MADISON
SUBJECT: MISTI IS GROUNDED

Dear Laurie,

Hello, I am Misti's mother. I am writing to you to tell you that Misti is not going to be able to meet you in the morning, because she needs to learn to honor her commitments and come home when she says she will. She is also not allowed to use the phone or computer, which is why you are getting this email from me.

Sincerely,

Wanda Pinkerton (Misti's mother)

"What do you mean, grounded?" Bud said when he saw Laurie the next morning. "You mean grounded grounded? For how long?"

"Beats me. I got an email from her *mom*," Laurie said, plunking down into the grass outside the school. She didn't know what they were going to do. They'd propped the pieces of floorboard together as well as they could the day before, but that gaping hole was going to be obvious to anyone who came into the shed. Someone would find it, and soon. If they hadn't already. And without Misti and her hot glue gun, they were doomed.

"But . . . ," Bud sputtered. "The hot glue gun!"

"I know." Laurie pulled up a tuft of grass and threw it on the ground.

"And . . . the exploring!" Bud groaned. "Can we explore without her? We can't, can we?" He looked at Laurie hopefully. "Can we?"

"We can't." Laurie picked at the hole in the ground left by the tuft. "It wouldn't be fair."

"What did her mom say, exactly?" Bud said. "Maybe you misinterpreted it."

Laurie rolled her eyes. "How am I supposed to remember exactly? She was grounded, not coming, blah blah. She needed to learn a lesson."

"Well, maybe she's coming to school for the lesson? Maybe that's what she meant?"

Laurie scowled. "That's not what she said, okay? It was crystal clear. Excuse me for not memorizing the email."

Bud rubbed his nose, making it wrinkle up like he had a snout. "I'd just feel better if I'd seen it, that's all. They have printers, Laurie. You could've used one."

Laurie stood up. Sometimes snouty Bud was more than she could take. "Fine, Bud. You can read it. We'll go to the library, and you can read it. We need to figure out what we're going to tell Miss Abernathy about our scavenger hunt plans anyway."

She stalked off toward the school building, kicking up little bits of turf as she went.

> **Good Reasons Not to Kill Bud Wallace**
> **by Laurie Madison, rising seventh grader**
> 1. Prison seventh grade probably even worse than regular seventh grade.
> 2. Murder definitely goes on permanent record.
> 3. Would have to come up with scavenger hunt ideas alone, which means dealing with Miss Abernathy alone.
> 4. Lots of good possibilities for revenge, which are not possible if he's dead.

"See? Are you happy now? It's just your basic email from your friend's weird mom. Okay?" Laurie stood next to the computer monitor in the school library, trying to keep it together. Like it wasn't bad enough that Bud totally doubted her email reading skills. No, he had to press the issue so she was forced to go into the school library, where 1. She had to be all nice and huggy kissy with Miss Lucille, the old lady librarian. 2. She had to dodge Candy Winkle and her tour of crazy people. And 3. She had to come face-to-face with Ponch and Jon, the bloodthirsty classroom gerbils she'd had to take care of last year, who were now summering in the school library. (It was probably technically face-to-face-to-face, but Laurie wasn't in any mood to get technical.)

It wasn't a great start to the day.

"Yeah, you're right. It looks like she's grounded." Bud said, after poring over the email for way more time than was necessary. It was what, three lines? Not much to pore over there.

"Yeah. No kidding."

"So what did you say?"

"What do you mean what did I say?" Laurie tried to keep her voice down, but she could tell she was sounding shrill. It was like she was doing a Misti impression. Miss Lucille had already turned her hearing aid down twice.

"In response. What did you write back?" Bud had taken on his I'm-talking-to-a-crazy-person tone.

Laurie gritted her teeth. "I didn't say anything back. Although, when you think about it, if she wants Misti to honor her commitments, she really should make her come meet us. You know, since she committed to that."

"Yeah, you should say that," Bud said.

"Really?" Laurie huffed.

"Sure." Bud shrugged.

"Okay, fine, I will." Laurie threw herself into the chair at the computer and started typing.

EMAIL

FROM: LAURIE MADISON

TO: MRS. PINKERTON

SUBJECT: Misti's grounding

Dear Mrs. Pinkerton,

Thank you for letting me know that Misti won't be coming today. But if she needs to learn to honor her commitments, shouldn't she be required to honor her commitment to Bud and myself?

Thank you,

Laurie Madison (Misti's friend)

Bud watched as Laurie hit send. Then he gave a low whistle. "Oh, man."

Laurie looked up. "What?"

"I can't believe you really sent it, that's all. I mean, you know."

Laurie shifted uncomfortably. "You know what?"

"Just that it's borderline disrespectful, that's all. You know. Mouthy. Fresh. Come on, Laurie, it's Misti's *mom*."

Laurie gaped at him, her mouth hanging open like she was a fish. "What? But you . . . it was your idea!"

Bud snickered. "Yeah, but I didn't think you'd *DO* it!"

Laurie grimaced and launched herself out of the chair and down the hallway.

What to Do When You've Been Tricked into Sending a Mouthy, Borderline Disrespectful Email to Your Friend's Mother
by Laurie Madison, rising seventh grader

1. Feign amnesia.
2. Pretend your account was hacked.
3. Throw yourself on Mrs. Pinkerton's mercy and beg forgiveness.
4. Make Bud pay.

It didn't take a brain surgeon to figure out where Laurie had gone. She wasn't outside and she wasn't inside, so Bud dodged Candy Winkle's latest tour group and headed for the shed.

Bud opened the door to the secret room slowly. Laurie

was slumped in the wing chair with the lion bookend in her lap. She was glaring at him.

"What a surprise, Bud Wallace exploring on his own. You're not supposed to do that, Bud," Laurie growled without moving.

"Yeah, what about you? Looks like you're in here too," Bud said.

Laurie didn't dignify that with an answer.

"Misti's mom probably won't think anything about that email, okay? I mean, she's Misti's mom, and Misti's not exactly the poster child for normal," Bud said, sitting on the other wing chair. He'd been right yesterday. It was much more comfortable than the stupid couch.

"You think?" Laurie still didn't move.

"She'll probably delete it by mistake instead of opening it." Bud gave a half grin.

Laurie put the lion bookend on the coffee table. "I hope so. I don't want to get Misti grounded for the next year and a half."

"Heck, she might even think it was polite. I mean, you did say 'dear' and 'thank you.' And you called her 'Mrs.'" Bud avoided Laurie's eyes. Even he couldn't make that last one sound plausible. He should've quit while he was ahead.

"Yeah, well, anyway, I wasn't exploring. I was just avoiding the tour group. Candy Winkle was on my tail the whole way out," Laurie grumbled.

"Me too. We might as well use this place while we have it though, right? Not to explore, but we can plan the scavenger hunt here, and then once Misti gets sprung we can do the real exploring."

"Okay. But hear this—I'm not willing to pin clues to bulletin boards." Laurie was putting her foot down there. She didn't care what Miss Abernathy said. She'd drop out before she did her lame clue ideas.

Bud nodded. "Me either." He'd been thinking about it, and he thought their only hope was throwing themselves on the mercy of Mrs. Hutchins or Principal Winkle. He was hoping they had a little more of Maria Tutweiler's ol' Tuckernuck Clucker spirit. And Mrs. Hutchins was supposed to be co-supervisor, right? So she could make official decisions.

"Believe me, Laurie, this scavenger hunt is cool and all, but if it starts going bad, I mean really bad, it's not worth it. I'm not willing to get a reputation as the Lame Clue Kid over it."

Laurie's mouth twitched. "Lame Clue Twins. Because if you go down, I go down too."

"Right." Bud snorted. "So no Lame Clue Twins."

Laurie gave Bud a half smile. "So that's what we'll do. We'll reject her ideas, but have some alternatives ready. Compromises, so they can't say we're being bad sports."

"And if things go south, we'll cut our losses and head for the hills." Bud held out his fist for Laurie to bump, and after a second's hesitation, she did. Nothing seals the deal like a good fist bump.

⌐

EMAIL
FROM: PRINCIPAL MARTIN WINKLE
TO: BETTY ABERNATHY AND OLIVIA HUTCHINS
SUBJECT: EMERGENCY MEETING
Today's *Morning News* is a disaster. Meet immediately in the staff room to talk strategy. We need to head this off ASAP.
Cancel all other meetings, plans, etc. This is your TOP PRIORITY.
Yours,
Martin Winkle
P.S. Could someone pick up doughnuts on the way?

⌐

"Okay, so we're agreed. We cross our fingers that Mrs.

Hutchins is in charge today, throw ourselves on her mercy, and ask for an extension." Bud put down the pencil. He and Laurie had tried to come up with "appropriate" compromise places for clues for what seemed like hours, but they couldn't agree on anything. And the things they could agree on were pretty much guaranteed to be nixed, unless the school safe or banister knobs were suddenly acceptable hiding places.

Laurie nodded. "And then you call Misti and see what's up at her house." There was no way she was making that phone call herself.

"Okay." Bud got up and went to shove his notes in his backpack, but as he unzipped it, Laurie made a hissing noise.

"What the—" Bud started.

"Shh!" Laurie hissed. "Listen!"

Bud pricked up his ears and felt the hairs on the back of his neck stand up. There were voices coming from behind the door in the corner. The door they hadn't investigated.

"Are they coming in here? Should we hide?" Bud said under his breath. Not that there were a lot of hiding places in the room. All anyone would have to do is open the door and they'd be caught. But he didn't think they had time to make it to the main door.

"Shh!" Laurie whispered again, not moving. They could still hear the voices, but they didn't seem to be getting any closer.

Laurie got to her feet and silently crept over to the passageway door. Then, with a significant look at Bud to keep his mouth shut, she opened it a crack.

The voices were louder now, but they didn't sound like voices in the passageway. They sounded farther away.

Laurie pulled the door open and stepped inside. It was dark, but up ahead she could see small, dim squares of light on the floor. She crept up to the first one and gasped.

"Bud!" she whispered. "Look!"

"What?" Bud did not want to get caught. He hurried forward and hoped Laurie knew what she was doing.

Things to Say If You're Caught Sneaking Around in a Hidden Room and/or Passageway
by Bud Wallace, rising seventh grader
1. Yeah, I just found this!
2. No, really! Just this second!

3. Nope, no idea it was here. I would've told you.
4. For real!

"What is it?" Bud asked, hurrying up to Laurie. He really hoped she wasn't flipping out. But it really looked like she was, because she was just standing staring at the wall.

Laurie pointed at the wall.

Afraid of what he was going to see, Bud looked at the wall where Laurie was pointing. And gasped.

It was the library. It was hazy, like they were looking through a screen or something, but it was definitely the school library, just on the other side of the wall. Miss Lucille was in there talking to Mrs. Hutchins, and they were leaning over something on the table. A paper or something. They both looked upset.

"Oh, man," Bud breathed. "Secret passageway?"

"It keeps going, too, farther that way," Laurie said, pointing down the passage. "We can see and hear everything they're doing."

"OH, MAN," Bud said, a little more loudly than he intended.

Mrs. Hutchins looked up and scanned the library,

then went back to the paper on the table.

"Oh, man," Bud said again, in a much softer voice. "This is so awesome." He pointed toward the corner of the library. "Look, you can see Ponch and Jon!"

Ponch and Jon were standing in their deluxe gerbil habitat, clenching their tiny fists and shaking with rage. It was like their gerbil superpowers had alerted them to Bud and Laurie's presence, but they were powerless to do anything but shriek and hop in fury.

"Where are we?"

"I think we must be on the other side of that weird abstract map on the wall in the library. It must be a secret screen or something," Laurie said. She couldn't believe it. She'd looked at the stupid map a thousand times and had never once suspected it was a secret viewing screen. "No wonder she kept all this secret," Laurie said. "I wonder where else this tunnel goes?"

"Misti's going to be ticked off if we go on without her," Bud said. Not that he really cared how ticked off Misti would be, but he thought it should be said.

"Shoot. You're right," Laurie said, deflating. They were totally exploring now. And Misti already had enough reasons to be mad at her, what with that email she'd sent her mom and all.

Bud turned to Laurie and put his hands on his hips. "We are *NOT* telling anyone about this. *ANY* of this," Bud said, sweeping his arm around at the tunnel and secret room. They just couldn't spill the beans now.

"No chance." Laurie folded her arms. It was one thing for her and Bud to secretly peek into the library. But the idea of someone like Betty Abernathy or Coach Burton or Principal Winkle peeking in was too horrible to imagine. No, there was no debate here. This was going to stay secret.

~

Bud checked his watch nervously. They'd lost track of time, and they were already five minutes late for their scavenger hunt meeting with Miss Abernathy or Mrs. Hutchins. So much for making a good impression.

They hurried over to Miss Abernathy's office, bracing themselves for a tongue-lashing, but it was empty. Miss Abernathy was nowhere to be seen.

"Oh, man, she must be really mad," Laurie breathed. "Maybe she's with Mrs. Hutchins?" They started toward Mrs. Hutchins's room at a half jog. The plan was to be obstinate about the hiding places, but not to tick the co-advisors off completely. Well, not yet, anyway.

They hustled down the hallway and darted into Mrs. Hutchins's room. It was empty.

Laurie and Bud stood staring at the empty classroom. Bud shrugged. "She must still be talking to Miss Lucille. That's weird," Bud said, hurrying in the direction of the library.

"Maybe they gave up on us?" Laurie said. She didn't think they'd give up after five minutes, but who knows, maybe they were teaching them a lesson about the importance of being punctual. It could happen.

Miss Lucille was by herself in the library, feeding Ponch and Jon an apple.

"We could ask?" Laurie said doubtfully, watching Miss Lucille through the glass in the door. She was holding the whole apple, letting Ponch and Jon take bites of it, not just dropping pieces of apple in the cage like people usually did.

"Naw, leave it," Bud said. Ponch and Jon seemed to be enjoying the personal attention. "Office?"

"Sure." Laurie shrugged. She was starting to feel really freaked out. It wasn't normal to go that long without running into someone, even if it was summer.

Bud reached for the office door just as Mrs. Hutchins hurried out. She jumped back when she saw them and laughed nervously. "Bud! Laurie! What are you doing here?"

Bud and Laurie exchanged a worried glance. "Scavenger hunt organizational meeting. Remember?"

"Oh, right, that." Mrs. Hutchins laughed again. It was a high-pitched, strained-sounding laugh. It didn't sound normal, especially since nothing was funny. "I'm sorry, kids, we'll have to reschedule. Things have gotten a little hectic here today. Why don't we plan on tomorrow? Or . . . you know what? I'm sure whatever ideas you've come up with are fine. Why don't you just go with those? Okay, thanks, great, bye." She hustled past them down the hall without a backward glance.

"What was that?" Laurie's eyes were wide.

"Well, something's definitely up," Bud said, staring after Mrs. Hutchins.

"All of our ideas are fine?" Laurie shook her head. "So if we went ahead with the plan to carve a clue into the ceiling of the library, they'd be okay with it?"

"Technically," Bud said. "But I really don't think we should do that one."

"Yeah, okay. But *TECHNICALLY*," Laurie said.

"Technically, yeah."

Laurie smiled. Maybe this wasn't going to be so bad after all.

Post-it note from Olivia Hutchins left on Betty Abernathy's computer

Betty—Just FYI, I canceled the meeting with the kids about the scavenger hunt. I told them to just trust their best instincts. They're good kids, I don't think we need to worry about them doing anything too crazy. We have other things to think about now.

Thanks,
Olivia

Post-it note on Olivia Hutchins's door from Betty Abernathy

Have you gone INSANE?
When was this?
Which way did they go?

Bud and Laurie had just walked down the school steps when a hand grabbed each of them from behind.

"You guys!" a voice gasped.

Misti pulled them backward and then bent over, hands on her knees, gasping for breath. "Seriously, I ran the whole way here. It's so crazy. You know I was grounded?"

Laurie cringed. "Yeah. About that. I'm really sorry about that email I sent your mom. That was totally out of line."

Misti waved her off. "No, that was genius. My mom is big on being consistent with her rules, so that meeting-my-commitments thing was perfect. I'd never have gotten out otherwise."

Laurie was taken aback. "Oh. Well, great."

"What's the big rush, though? Why are you all out of breath?" Bud said, bending over to look Misti in the face. She was turning a strange hot pink, kind of like her head was about to explode.

"You haven't seen it, then?" Misti gasped, straightening up. She pulled a folded newspaper out of her back pocket and smacked Bud in the chest with it. "LeFranco.

He wasn't bluffing."

Bud unfolded the newspaper and looked at the head-line. Then he passed it to Laurie in shock.

"Oh, man."

Laurie looked at the headline. Whatever she'd been afraid of, this was worse.

MARIA TUTWEILER'S FILTHY LIFE OF CRIME
BOOTLEGGER! COUNTERFEITER! THIEF! MURDERER!

Beloved founder of Tuckernuck Hall was secretly a hardened criminal and the bloodthirsty killer of Marchetti the Magician.

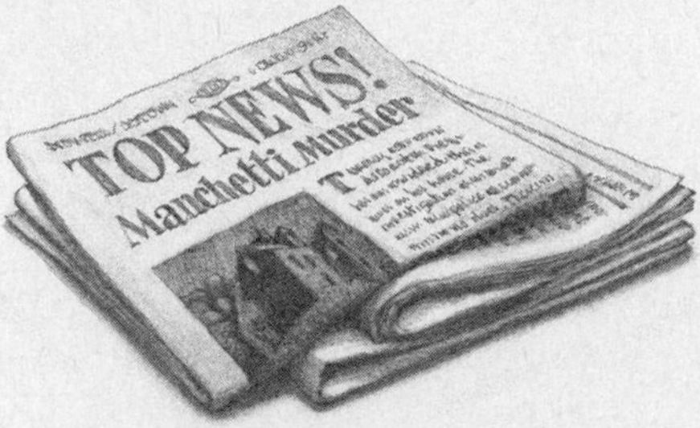

PART THREE

THE MARCHETTI CASE

MARIA TUTWEILER'S FILTHY LIFE OF CRIME

BOOTLEGGER! COUNTERFEITER! THIEF! MURDERER!

Beloved founder of Tuckernuck Hall was secretly a hardened criminal and the bloodthirsty killer of Marchetti the Magician.

As part of our investigative report, the *Morning News* has uncovered irrefutable evidence that Maria Tutweiler, founder of the controversial Tuckernuck Hall Intermediate School, was actually a bootlegger, thief, forger, and master criminal—and was also behind one of the bloodiest and most brutal murders of the twentieth century: the murder of Alphonse Marchetti, best known as Marchetti the Magician.

See page 2.

"Is it as bad as it sounds?" Bud was slumped on the steps with his head in his hands.

"Worse," Laurie said, staring blankly at the newspaper.

"Well, it's not true," Bud said.

"Of course it's not true," Laurie said. "But it's still in the paper."

"They really have evidence?" Bud said, still not looking up.

"There's a photo of Maria Tutweiler entering Alphonse Marchetti's house on the night he was murdered. It's on the front page. And there's another one of her with a cop, getting questioned, it looks like."

Bud groaned. "So she's really a bootlegging murderous thieving thiever?"

Laurie folded the paper. "Well, that's what LeFranco says, but he's going to have a hard time convincing me that Maria Tutweiler committed a brutal and bloody murder. It's not her style."

Bud snorted. "Well, great. We'll just tell them that it's not her style, and I'm sure they'll drop the whole thing." Bud lay back on the steps. It was a bad move—the steps were really uncomfortable, but once he'd done it, he felt like he had to commit to it.

"Fine, excuse me." Laurie tried to fold the newspaper again, but it was too thick.

"Seriously, what are we going to do? If they think she was a murderer, nobody will want to come to Tuckernuck. They'll shut down the school for sure." Bud tried not to squirm his shoulders. He hadn't gone through all that trouble to find the treasure and save the school just to have it shut down over a newspaper story.

"I don't know, Bud. Maybe not. Maybe people will think he's crazy." Laurie stood up. "Anyway, we'll defend her somehow. That's all there is to it. She's innocent, we'll defend her, case closed. LeFranco's just a dog chewing off our ankles." She frowned. That wasn't right. But she couldn't remember exactly what her dad had said, and chewing off their ankles sure felt like what LeFranco was doing.

Memo left by Betty Abernathy in the school mailboxes of Bud Wallace and Laurie Madison

RE: The Scavenger Hunt
Mr. Wallace and Miss Madison:
  I understand you spoke with Mrs. Hutchins today and she said that you no longer need to clear your "ideas" for the scavenger hunt with us before

implementing them. Believe me when I say
this was an error on her part.
   YOU MUST CLEAR ALL SCAVENGER
HUNT CLUES WITH US FIRST. DO NOT
hide any clues without our approval. DO
NOT prepare any hiding places without our
approval. DO NOT make any plans without
our approval.
   Please see me at your first opportunity
to discuss when we can reschedule our
organizational meeting.
   Thank you,
   Betty Abernathy

"How's Misti doing?"

Laurie shielded her eyes against the sun and peered into the school yard. "I don't see her. She must be close to finished, though. She was really going crazy with that glue gun."

After she'd shown them the article, Misti had stomped off to the shed to start gluing the trapdoor back together. Laurie just hoped that there would still be some way inside once she'd gotten done gluing everything in sight.

Bud just grunted. Laurie stared at him for a long minute and then smacked him on the knee.

"For Pete's sake, Bud, snap out of it, okay? We'll fix this."

Bud nodded. "You know, this LeFranco stuff, trying to clear Maria Tutweiler's name?" he started, and then hesitated. Laurie raised her eyebrows at him. "It's just . . . it's going to take a lot of time."

Laurie shrugged. "Yeah. But we need to do it."

"It's going to take time away from the scavenger hunt. I mean, a lot of time."

Laurie rolled her eyes at Bud. "Bud, seriously. The scavenger hunt?"

Bud frowned. "Yeah?"

"That scavenger hunt is pretty much dead in the water at this point, right? I mean, Betty Abernathy isn't going to let us do *anything*."

Bud grinned. "You figured that out too?"

Laurie shook her head. "I figure, we keep pretending we're doing it, to throw her off, right? And so we don't lose access to the school."

"Right, and we'll do what we can with it." Bud gave a sly nod.

"But we've got to focus on the important stuff. Saving

Maria Tutweiler's butt," Laurie finished.

"Again," Bud added.

"AGAIN." Laurie smirked. "So, do you think you can meet up after dinner?"

"What, tonight?" Bud sat up. It felt like the stairs had left a permanent indentation in his back. "I think so. Why?"

"Good. We need to start doing a little investigating ourselves. Find out what LeFranco is talking about and who that guy was she supposedly killed. Then we'll meet back in the secret room." She laughed a dry, barky laugh. "I mean, it's secret for a reason, right? Maybe there's evidence in there that we can use to clear her. But first we have to have the facts."

Bud nodded. It was something, at least. "Got it. We'll have her cleared in no time."

~

EMAIL

FROM: CANDY WINKLE

TO: PRINCIPAL MARTIN WINKLE

SUBJECT: Tutweiler Tours

Hi, Pookie, the good news is that the tour bookings haven't fallen off at all. In fact, there may be even more interest now than there was.

The bad news is that some of the people signing up are asking if the murder site is going to be included on the tour.

Kisses,

Candy

P. S. Our tour fan signed up again.

EMAIL

FROM: PRINCIPAL MARTIN WINKLE

TO: CANDY WINKLE

SUBJECT: Tuckernuck Hall

Sweetie Pie,

I'm glad the tours are still doing well. That's very reassuring. Unfortunately, I've already had calls from parents who aren't sure they want their kids going to a "murderer's school." I'm going to speak with the people at the *Daily Herald* today and see if we can't get in front of this whole thing.

Keep an eye on that tour fan. I'm having misgivings about him.

Hugs,

Pookie Bear

Headline in the Daily Herald, *competitor of the Morning News*

MARTIN WINKLE DISMISSES SCURRILOUS RUMORS

Principal Martin Winkle expressed disgust today at recent allegations against Tucker-nuck Hall Intermediate School founder Maria Tutweiler. "The charges are simply ridiculous," said Winkle. "There is absolutely no truth to them, and people should consider the source." Winkle was alluding to the conflict that arose last year when former school board president and current *Morning News* editor-in-chief Walker LeFranco failed in his attempt to have Tuckernuck Hall closed and the building demolished.

Article continues on page 5.

"I didn't want to say anything in front of Laurie, but maybe we should take another look at Hamilton Junior High?"

Laurie stopped on her way past the kitchen and listened. She'd been in the den, trying to find whatever
she could on Alphonse Marchetti and Maria Tutweiler's
nefarious past, but there was only so much she could
get printed out with her brother, Jack, bugging her to
let him get online to play World of Warcraft. It's pretty
much impossible to get any secret investigating done
when someone's hovering over your shoulder.

Laurie clenched the few pages she'd managed to print
in her fists and edged closer to the kitchen door.

"Are you serious?" Laurie's mother sounded like she
was putting dishes in the dishwasher. "We went through
this last year. We're a family of proud Tuckernuck
Cluckers. You don't really think she's a murderer, do
you?"

"Of course not." Laurie's father sounded grim. "But
it doesn't matter what I think. It matters what the people
in the town think. That school was just getting back on
its feet. If people decide not to send their kids there . . ."

"Which is exactly what you're doing." Laurie's mother
shut the dishwasher with a bang. Being a Tuckernuck
Clucker was something she took seriously.

"No, I just don't want to be caught by surprise if the
school shuts down suddenly. We don't need that stress

again. It's summer now, so it's a good time to be thinking about this kind of thing." Laurie's dad paused. "It's
not like she doesn't have friends at Hamilton. Kimmy
goes there, and they used to be best friends."

Laurie stifled a snort. Used to be was right. She and
Kimmy hadn't been close ever since Kimmy joined up
with the popular crowd at Hamilton. As much as Laurie
had begged to go to Hamilton last year, it was the last
thing she wanted to do now.

"Well, I hope you're wrong. I can't imagine people
will believe one silly article."

Laurie could hear her mother opening the refrigera-
tor. "Who wants pie?" her mom yelled from the kitchen.

Laurie unfroze and quickly hurried past the door and
up the stairs. "I do!" Laurie called down, once she was
safely in her room. It was a lie, though. The way her
stomach was churning, she didn't think she'd be able to
eat a single bite.

~~

Bud was waiting for the pages he'd found to finish
printing when his dad came up behind him. He was
watching the printer, which was super slow, so he
didn't even realize his dad was there until he felt a hand
on his shoulder.

"What's this you're looking up?"

Bud almost hit the ceiling, but he managed to smile back at his dad. He didn't want to come off like a jumpy freak, even if he was one.

"Oh, I was just looking up some stuff."

His dad picked up the papers from the printer. "Alphonse Marchetti?" His dad looked confused. "This isn't for the scavenger hunt, is it?"

Bud shifted uncomfortably. "I was just looking him up because of that stuff in the paper. You know."

"I must've missed that article." Bud's dad frowned. Bud wasn't surprised, actually. They didn't get the *Morning News*, and Bud sure as heck wasn't about to suggest that his dad read the article about his school's murderous founder.

"Oh, it's stupid. Just some stuff about Maria Tutweiler, you know."

Bud's dad's frown deepened. "No, I don't know. Is it something I should see?" He turned and called into the other room. "Flora? Did you see an article today about Maria Tutweiler?"

Bud groaned inwardly. Flora Downey was the music teacher at Tuckernuck Hall, and she and his dad had been seeing each other since the beginning of the year. Which meant that Bud had been seeing her, too. A whole lot of her. Way more of her than he wanted to.

Flora Downey came into the office from the living room, carrying a couple of foreign artsy-type DVDs. She was wearing a T-shirt and shorts. Bud tried to avert his eyes. There was just something very wrong about seeing a teacher in shorts.

"You're not taking that article seriously, are you, Wally?" Miss Downey rolled her eyes. "It's ridiculous."

"What? What did it say? It looks like I'm the only one who didn't read it." Mr. Wallace gave a half smile, but Bud could tell he was concerned. He was always concerned when it came to school stuff.

"Just some ridiculous accusations, claiming she's responsible for everything from the stock market crash to the Kennedy assassination to the Great Chicago Fire."

Bud was glad she'd put it that way, instead of listing the things Maria Tutweiler had actually been accused of doing. It sounded crazier Miss Downey's way.

"She wasn't even alive for all of those," Bud said, fixing his eyes on Miss Downey's sandals. Sandals that exposed her toes. A kid should never have to see a teacher's toes.

"Exactly." Miss Downey smiled at Bud. "Now, which

of these do you want to see?" Miss Downey held up two
super-serious-looking movies with pictures of gloomy
people on the covers. One was in Swedish and the other
one was in Japanese. Bud sighed. Family movie night
was going to kill him.

"They both look really good," Bud's dad said. "But
what about this article? Is this going to hurt Bud's future,
if colleges associate him with a criminal?"

"Of course not. It's just muckraking, that's all it is.
Nothing to worry about." Miss Downey smiled. "Guess
I get to be the deciding vote. Swedish it is!"

Note from Mrs. Wanda Pinkerton to Mr. Mel Pinkerton

Mel—While you're out could you pick me up some
more glue for the hot glue gun? I don't know
how I've managed to go through it all so fast.
Also, pick up some glitter and hot pink sequins. I
want to bedazzle that new sweatshirt I picked up
for Misti.
Thanks,
Wanda

Quote under a Life *magazine photo of the magician Alphonse Marchetti*

"All of my secrets are within the Marchetti Bird.
She can tell you all the tales of my life."
Alphonse Marchetti

Bud looked at the *Life* magazine printout that Laurie had made and shook his head. "Why can't anything be straightforward with this guy? What the heck is this supposed to mean?"

Laurie shrugged. "He was a magician. Magicians are supposed to be mysterious."

"I guess. Did you mostly find out stuff about the bird, then?" Bud handed the printout back to Laurie.

Laurie nodded. "Pretty much. Did you find anything out about the murder?"

Bud made a face. "Yeah. It's pretty gross."

"Great." A murder was bad enough, but a gross murder was going to be hard to take. Laurie had a weak stomach when it came to that kind of thing.

Laurie leaned up against the shed. "Misti's coming, right?" It was starting to get dark outside, and the whole yard was looking a little spooky. She wasn't used to seeing the school except in full daylight, and there seemed to be more shadows than there should've been.

Bud wasn't worried about the shadows. He was just happy he wasn't watching another Swedish movie about people who didn't seem to do anything but have long discussions and die. He'd seen enough of those to last a lifetime.

"She'll be here. She said something about a bedazzling accident. She might be a little late."

Laurie stared at him. "A bedazzling accident? What's that?"

"Beats me." Bud said, watching something moving in the distance. "Wait, I think that's her."

Misti appeared at the edge of the school yard. She didn't look happy.

Laurie sucked in her breath. "Wow. I think I know what a bedazzling accident is."

Misti was wearing a big gray sweatshirt with her shorts and T-shirt, and it looked like a crafts store had exploded all over it. Laurie could see sequins, lace, glitter, lamé, and a bunch of other things she didn't even know the names of. It wasn't a look that even Misti could pull off.

"Not a word," Misti said, stalking past them and

jerking open the door to the shed.

"I wasn't going to say anything, I swear." Laurie bit her lip. Giggling would not go over well right now.

"Believe it or not, I got off lucky. My sister Tiffi got a jumpsuit. *A JUMPSUIT.* I don't even know how my mom managed to find one. We're planning to spill grape juice in the near future." Misti inspected the trapdoor. She'd glued a big piece of scrap plywood over the hole, so it looked terrible, but not like a secret passageway. "The hot glue seems to have done the job, though." She gave Laurie a small smile. "Maybe Maria Tutweiler has some spare clothes in there."

Possible Acts of Vengeance for the
Bedazzled Sweatshirt
by Misti Pinkerton, rising seventh grader,
with assistance from Laurie Madison
and Bud Wallace
1. Bedazzled Mother's Day gift.
2. Bedazzled birthday gift.
3. Bedazzled Christmas gift.
4. Bedazzled Valentine's Day gift.
5. Bedazzled Thanksgiving gift.

6. Bedazzled Fourth of July gift.
7. Bedazzled Labor Day gift.
8. Join punk band, bedazzle self.

It was Misti who first noticed that something was wrong with the room.

She grabbed Laurie's arm just as Bud plunked his backpack down onto one of the wing chairs. "Bud, stop. Look."

Bud froze. He didn't know what she was talking about, but he knew it wasn't good. She looked deadly serious, even with her sequins reflecting light onto her face. It made her look like she had disco chicken pox and didn't find it amusing.

"What is it?"

"Somebody's been here." Misti's voice was hushed.

Bud and Laurie looked around nervously. "Are you sure?" Laurie whispered. "How can you tell?"

Misti pointed at the desk in the corner. "Did you put the ledger I was looking at away? Because it's gone."

Laurie hurried over to the desk and looked. Misti was right. The ledger was now propped neatly, with some folders, at the back of the desk.

"Oh, man," Laurie breathed, scanning the room. "The lion. The lion bookend. Look."

The last time Laurie had seen the lion bookend was when she put it down on the coffee table. Now it was back on the shelf. Right where it had been when she first found it.

"What's that about?" Laurie hugged her arms around herself. She didn't want to touch anything.

"Well, that's super creepy," Bud whispered. "What does that mean? Somebody comes in here?"

"Or it's a ghost," Misti said slowly. "This is an old house. A ghost could live here. Maybe it likes its room just so."

"Well, whatever it is, I'm done. Let's get out of here," Bud said, zipping his book bag shut.

Laurie shook her head. She wasn't going to let herself get scared away at the first sign of something weird. It was way too late for that. This whole thing was weird. "No way. And go where? It was hard enough getting permission to come out tonight. I don't want to waste it."

Bud stared at his book bag. She had a point. All he had waiting for him at home was that Swedish movie. If he went home now, he'd be expected to join in the family movie time and post-movie discussion. Miss Downey loved to discuss.

"All right. But don't touch anything. And it goes without saying, we ditch the exploring idea." Bud hesitated. "And at the first sign of trouble, we get the heck out. Agreed?"

"Agreed." Laurie perched on one of the chairs. Her neck felt all prickly. She didn't think Misti was right about it being a ghost, but she didn't know what else it could be. She really didn't get the sense that Principal Winkle was spending his off hours in the secret room.

"I don't think the ghost would mind if we used it," Misti said, sitting down on the footstool and pulling her bedazzled sweatshirt over her head. "Especially if it's Maria Tutweiler! Do you think it's her? Maybe we could get a Ouija board and she could help us!"

Unless she's really a murderer, Bud thought. But he didn't say it out loud. Instead he just shook his head. "It's not Maria Tutweiler, okay? And it's not a ghost. It's just some weird thing. A person. Or a scientific phenomenon. Or we're wrong, and we just forgot moving things. But it doesn't matter, we'll just share our info and leave. Please, Misti?" His voice cracked. He wasn't going to be able to do this if she kept talking about ghosts all night.

He was creeped out enough as it was.

"Fine," Misti said. "What did you find out?"

"It's pretty gross," Bud said, pulling his papers out. "Apparently Marchetti was this really famous magician a gazillion years ago, right? He did illusions, plus a lot of things with some bird prop. And he was supposedly involved in all this bad stuff, like organized crime. And the feds were going to arrest him, but the crime bosses, they wanted to get him first. And he just laughed it all off. Then the night that the police were planning to arrest him, he did a show downtown at the Celestial Theatre, and one of the things in his act was a disappearing act, where he makes his assistant disappear. Except that night, he switched it around and made *himself* disappear instead. And he never reappeared."

Misti frowned. "How is this a murder? It sounds like he skipped town."

Bud shook his head. "That's what the cops thought, but no one saw him leave backstage. So they went to his house, and when they got there, it was completely trashed, and there was blood everywhere. Like, tons of it. I didn't print out the picture I found of the scene, because it was really bad. *CSI*-type stuff."

Bud swallowed hard. He hadn't realized quite how

much blood people had inside. He'd almost barfed on the keyboard.

"So how is Maria Tutweiler involved?" Laurie said, leaning forward.

"Beats me. I know she knew him, but I don't know why she would kill him. LeFranco had those pictures, though. Maybe her fingerprints are on the murder weapon or something."

Laurie bit her lip. "LeFranco said she was into boot-legging—you know, alcohol smuggling, that kind of thing. That would fit, wouldn't it? Wouldn't that mean she was mixed up with organized crime?"

Bud shrugged again. "Maybe. I hadn't thought of that." The secret room was starting to make a whole lot more sense, and in a really bad way.

"I didn't find anything about bootlegging, though. I mostly found pictures of him and the Marchetti Bird." Laurie passed the picture from *Life* magazine to Misti. "That's the Marchetti Bird there—that's what they called it. It was almost as famous as he was, apparently. He used it in his act, and no one ever could figure out how it worked."

Misti examined the picture. "That quote . . . did he really say that? About the bird holding all his secrets?"

Laurie nodded and scooted over next to Misti on the footstool. "Yeah, but no one knew what he meant. Apparently it was some kind of mechanical bird, but you couldn't see any of the works, it just looked like smooth metal. But he could make it open its wings and beak and sing and all sorts of stuff."

Bud whistled. "That's pretty cool."

"Yeah, according to this stuff, he was a really good magician. He wasn't doing kids' parties or whatever, he headlined big theaters. And the Marchetti Bird was a big part of it. He took it everywhere. And when he was murdered, it disappeared and was never seen again."

Misti peered at the picture. "I wish this picture wasn't so bad. How big was it? No offense, Laurie, but your family needs to get a decent printer."

"Sorry about that. It was pretty big—bigger than a regular bird." Laurie's eyes roamed the room to find something to compare it to. "Oh, hey! It looked a lot like . . ."

Laurie went cold.

"Like what?" Misti elbowed her in the ribs, but Laurie didn't move.

"Like what, Laurie?" Bud was almost afraid to ask. All the color had drained from Laurie's face, and she looked like she was going to throw up.

Without a word, Laurie got up and walked to the cabinet next to the couch. Then she opened the lattice door in the front and stood next to it.

"Like this bird." She reached inside the cabinet and pulled out a large metal bird. She put it down on the coffee table, and the cold, smooth metal reflected the overhead lights and made it look like it was shimmering. "Holy cow, guys," Laurie breathed. "I think this is the Marchetti Bird."

What to Do When You Find Proof That the Founder of Your School Is an Evil Murderer by Laurie Madison, rising seventh grader and future Hamilton Junior High student
1. Cry.
2. Turn it over to cops, wash your hands of the whole thing, and become a Hamilton Junior High student.
3. Cry some more.
4. Become completely irrational.

"I don't care! Just because she had the bird doesn't mean she killed him!" Laurie felt like throttling Bud. He was always such a downer.

"You mean the bird he never went anywhere with-out?" Bud said drily.

"Yeah."

"You mean the bird that disappeared when he was murdered?"

"Yeah."

"You mean the bird that's been hidden in her secret room that NO ONE ELSE KNOWS ABOUT?" Bud crossed his arms.

"Yeah." Laurie crossed hers too.

"Yeah, I can see why you'd think she's innocent." Bud rolled his eyes. "Look, I don't like this either, Laurie, but face facts! It's PROOF, okay?"

Laurie shook her head. "Sorry, but I'm going to need a little more than that."

"Uh, Laurie?" Misti's voice was tentative. She was sitting on the floor next to the cabinet holding a small carved box. "You might want to take a look at this."

"What's that?" Laurie grumbled. She wasn't going to let herself be sidetracked.

"Just look. This box was in the same cabinet with the bird, down on the shelf with the ledgers." Misti held it out to Laurie.

Laurie took it slowly. Misti looked sad and apologetic,

like she was just about to kick Laurie's dog but felt really bad about it. It gave Laurie a sick feeling.

Laurie looked into the box. There wasn't much stuff in there, just an ancient wallet-type thing and some boring-looking documents.

Laurie pulled out the wallet and looked at Misti. "You are not serious."

"I'm really sorry, Laurie." Misti blinked and looked away.

Laurie put the box down on the coffee table next to the Marchetti Bird and opened the wallet. There were a couple of ancient-looking dollars, a library card, and a driver's license. And a membership card to the Society of American Magicians. Belonging to Mr. Alphonse Marchetti.

PART FOUR
HARD EVIDENCE

Bud fanned out the cards on the coffee table like he was in a casino. "Okay, so we've got a driver's license made out to Alphonse Marchetti. A membership card for some club in Washington, D.C., signed by Alphonse Marchetti. The Society of American Magicians membership card, signed by society president Houdini for member Alphonse Marchetti. And some kind of business card thing, with a picture of Magician Alphonse Marchetti *and* the Marchetti Bird. I don't see that there's any doubt that it's his wallet."

Laurie didn't move; she just sat slumped in the chair, glaring at Bud's card arrangement. "Okay, fine, but she could have stolen it. Didn't LeFranco say she's a thief? Maybe she was a notorious pickpocket." Laurie wasn't willing to give in yet. She knew what it was like to be framed. If Betty Abernathy had had her way when they found the treasure, she and Bud would be sitting in jail cells right now.

Bud threw up his hands in disgust, almost smacking Misti in the head by mistake. He stood up. "You talk to her, Misti. She's not listening to me."

Misti picked up the membership card and inspected it. It was dated 1926 and looked even older than the rest of the stuff. "Is that the real Houdini? *The* Harry Houdini's real signature? This must be worth something."

Laurie made a weird noise in the back of her throat. "Everything in here is worth something, Misti! Look around! I don't know why you guys are so convinced she's a murderer. Everyone thought she was insane last year, remember? And that wasn't true. There's got to be some explanation."

Laurie went back to slumping and stared at the floor. This was the last thing she'd expected to find out when she suggested they do some investigating. She wished they'd never found the stupid room.

"Okay, how's this?" Bud said, sitting down again. "We don't know what this all means. It could mean LeFranco's right and she's a murderer. It could mean something else. But that's not important now, right?"

"Huh? Of course it is," Laurie had always known it would happen someday. Bud had totally lost it. Not important. Laurie snorted.

"I think it matters, Bud," Misti said, looking up from her inspection of the Houdini signature. "Sheesh."

"But not really!" Bud explained. "Whether it's true or not, what we need to do now is decide what to do. Do we turn this stuff over to the police as evidence? Or do we hide it and protect her?"

Laurie and Misti exchanged a glance. Bud was making a certain amount of sense.

"I for one vote to hide it," Bud went on. "LeFranco has whatever evidence he has. We don't need to give him any more. I don't want to be the one responsible for ruining Maria Tutweiler's name and shutting down the school."

"You just want to keep the secret room." Laurie folded her arms. "It has nothing to do with LeFranco."

Bud got a shifty-eyed look on his face. "Well, yeah. But so what? It's cool!"

Misti stacked the ID cards back up. "I think he's right. We don't need to tell anyone about this." She put the cards back into the wallet and then stroked the head of the Marchetti Bird. "And maybe if we're lucky, we can convince his bird to tell us all his secrets."

Laurie rolled her eyes. "Right, you work on that. Okay,

fine, who cares, we'll keep it secret. And when Winkle busts us, you can be the one who does the explaining."

If he busted them. Now that they had evidence to hide, keeping the room secret didn't seem like such a terrible idea. But she wasn't about to let Bud know that, not since he'd been so quick to turn on Maria Tutweiler.

"Great!" Bud popped up like a cork. "So what I was thinking was—"

"Bud! Shh!" Misti grabbed his knee. She was aiming for his arm, but the jumping up took her by surprise.

Misti sat stock-still for a second, listening. Then she gave a triumphant squeal. "I knew it was a ghost!"

"What are you talking about?" Laurie wasn't in the mood to be patient.

"Listen!" Misti pointed randomly into the air. It was hard to pinpoint the location of the ghost.

Bud and Laurie both listened intently, cocking their heads like a pack of curious dogs. Finally Bud shook his head. "It's not a ghost. It's the voices again."

"Miss Lucille?" Laurie got up quietly.

"I don't think so. Come on." Bud crept over to the passageway door and put his hand on the knob.

"Wait!" Laurie hissed. "Remember, someone was in

here. The lion bookend moved! What if they're coming this way?"

Bud turned the knob and opened the door. "Then we run for it. But I think they're in the library."

The three of them crept slowly down the passageway, listening intently as the voices got louder.

"Definitely not Miss Lucille," Laurie whispered.

When they got to the screen in the library, they peered out into the darkened room, scanning the area.

"There's nobody in there," Bud said, disappointed. Ponch and Jon were even asleep. He had been sure the voices would be coming from the library. It didn't make any sense.

"It's because it's a ghost," Misti said.

"It's not a ghost," Laurie said. "It's just farther down the passage."

She crept on into the darkness, more carefully since she didn't know what was up ahead.

After another turn in the passageway, Laurie saw soft light coming from another screen up ahead. The voices were much louder now.

"This is it," Laurie said, creeping up to the screen and peeking through. And then she froze. "Oh, man, you guys," she breathed. "You're not going to believe this."

> ### First Thoughts When Peeking Through the Screen
> **by Laurie Madison, rising seventh grader**
> No way, is that Walker LeFranco? What's he doing in TUCKERNUCK HALL?

> ### First Thoughts When Peeking Through the Screen
> **by Bud Wallace, rising seventh grader**
> Is that Reginald the Janitor? What's he doing here? And who's that other guy?

> ### First Thoughts When Peeking Through the Screen
> **by Misti Pinkerton, future ghost hunter**
> Aw, crud, they're alive!

"What's going on?" Bud didn't understand who Reginald was talking to or why he looked so secretive about it. The guy Reginald was with looked familiar, but if he had to keep track of all the grown-ups in town, Bud wouldn't have room in his brain for anything else.

"LeFranco. That's LeFranco," Laurie whispered.

"Wayne LeFranco? The dead one?" Misti perked up hopefully.

Laurie gave her a look. "No, Walker LeFranco. The alive one, Misti."

"Crud." Misti slouched back down. That's what she'd thought, but she figured it was worth asking.

"That doesn't make sense. Why would LeFranco be here?" Bud wiped his nose and turned into snouty Bud. Laurie had to look away.

"Shut it for a second and maybe we'll find out."

Bud snorted in irritation, but he shut his mouth.

Reginald was the janitor at Tuckernuck Hall, and he was a real stickler about where you could bring your liquids and that kind of thing. He'd been pretty suspicious of Laurie and Misti ever since last September's unfortunate orange juice incident. Laurie and Misti couldn't see him in the halls without him doing that "I'm watching you" sign, where he pointed two fingers at his eyes and then pointed at them. It was getting old, to be honest.

Laurie wasn't the least bit surprised to see him in the school. But Walker LeFranco was another story. He hated everything about Tuckernuck Hall and had always sworn he'd never set foot in the place. (That wasn't an exact quote. His version used lots of what Misti called "cuss jar words.") But he definitely seemed to be setting foot in it now.

"Now we're all clear about tomorrow? You know what to do?" LeFranco paced in front of Reginald. "I don't want to have to clean up your mess."

Reginald nodded. "Yes, sir, I know what to do."

"Good. You won't need to say much, and if you run into any problems, just refer people to me. Might be good to take a few days off. Now have you been looking around here, like I said?"

Reginald shifted his weight uncomfortably. "I have, but I haven't located any of the things you asked about. No secret whatnots anywhere around here. I thought the back storage room might work for the story, though."

"Nothing? What have you been doing all this time?" LeFranco barked angrily. "Well, if that's what we've got, that's what we'll have to go with, but I think you should try to look a little harder, Reginald. I'm doing you a favor here. Don't forget that."

"No, sir, I won't forget." Reginald didn't look anything like he usually looked at school. At school, he was always plowing through the hallways, ready to take down any juvenile offenders and smacking mouthy kids in the butt with his dust rag. He looked much smaller talking to LeFranco, somehow.

Laurie turned away. "What's going on? What are they talking about?"

Bud shook his head. He didn't like the look of this one bit. "I don't know. But we'll find out."

What We Know
by Laurie Madison, Bud Wallace, and Misti Pinkerton, rising seventh graders

1. Someone has found the secret room.
2. Or there's a ghost. (Added by Misti Pinkerton.)
3. That someone is not Reginald.
4. Unless he was lying to LeFranco, which is possible. (Added by Bud Wallace.)
5. But not likely. (Added by Laurie Madison.)
6. CONCLUSION: We know nothing.

Headline in the Morning News

TUCKERNUCK SCHOOL JANITOR UNCOVERS EVIDENCE OF FOUNDER'S GUILT

Reginald Moore, longtime janitor at Tuckernuck Hall Intermediate School, has uncovered evidence that will prove once and for all that Maria Tutweiler murdered famed magician Alphonse Marchetti many years ago. In a special press conference to be held at three o'clock today, *Morning News* Editor-in-Chief Walker LeFranco and Reginald Moore will appear to present this incontrovertible proof to the media and put to rest any questions about this foul woman once and for all.

"Isn't *he* the media?" Misti said the next morning when they met up outside the school. "How can he present proof to the media when he is the media?"

Laurie shrugged. "He's the editor-in-chief. He can do pretty much whatever he wants." Laurie nodded toward Misti's unbedazzled T-shirt. "Nice. How'd you get away with that?"

Misti grinned. "Grape juice accident. I don't think that sweatshirt's ever going to be the same." Misti stopped grinning. "Heads up." Laurie looked across the lawn in time to see Calliope Judkin walk up the steps and head inside. "Bet she's going to see Reginald."

Misti nodded. "Bet he's not going to want to see her."

> ### Note to Self
> ### by Calliope Judkin
> Laurie Madison and Misti Pinkerton at school again, obviously on Reginald stakeout. What are they waiting for? Highly suspicious. Must investigate. NO DISTRACTIONS.

EMAIL

FROM: CANDY WINKLE

TO: PRINCIPAL MARTIN WINKLE

SUBJECT: Today's Tours

Well, Cutie Pie, it looks like we've got a problem. About half of the people in the afternoon tour have canceled. I can't help but think that it's because of that horrible LeFranco man's article. What should we do?

Hugs,

Candy

P.S. Of course that weird little man didn't cancel.

EMAIL

FROM: PRINCIPAL MARTIN WINKLE

TO: CANDY WINKLE

SUBJECT: No need to fear

Honey Bunny,

I don't think we should worry just yet. When the merchandise stops selling, then I'll worry.

Love,

Your Sweet Patootie Pie

EMAIL

FROM: JANET DAVIS AT TUCKERNUCK HALL GIFT SHOP

TO: PRINCIPAL MARTIN WINKLE

SUBJECT: Merchandise sales

Principal Winkle,

I just thought you should know that we've had a rash of people returning their I HEART MARIA TUTWEILER shirts this morning and demanding refunds. I don't know whether the fit is bad or what, but I thought you should know.

Thanks,

Janet in the gift shop

EMAIL

FROM: PRINCIPAL MARTIN WINKLE

TO: CANDY WINKLE

SUBJECT: Second Thoughts

Okay, I'm worried.

⌇

Laurie and Misti were sprawled on the grass when Bud hurried up, looking around anxiously.

Laurie peered up at him. "What's up, Bud?"

"Did you guys go to the shed yet this morning?" He didn't look at them. He scanned the horizon like he was watching for a ship or something.

Laurie shook her head. "No. Not yet. We were waiting for you."

"Well, I went there. And this was stuck in the door."

Bud reached down and handed Laurie a bright orange piece of paper, and then plunked down onto the grass.

Laurie stared down at the paper in her hands. "What do you mean, it was stuck in the door? Like, accidentally? Or on purpose?" Laurie didn't even want to unfold the paper. The longer she went without knowing what it was, the better.

"On purpose. Wedged inside. Like someone knew we'd been going there. It's addressed to you, incidentally.

Well, both of us, I guess."

Laurie carefully unfolded the paper and looked at it. It was a note.

> TO THE KIDS WHO FOUND THE TREASURE.
> I need your help. You have information that can help me. I have information that can help you. Name the time and place, and we can meet.
> Signed,
> A Friend

"Um, no?" Laurie felt really weirded out. She didn't care how much this person was "a friend," there was no way she was meeting them. "How about never? How about the time is never and the place is nowhere on earth?"

Bud nodded his head. He had his whole crazy face going on. "Yeah, I'm not about to meet that person."

"It's too bad it doesn't say Buck and Loni, because then we'd know it was Candy Winkle," Laurie said.

"Yeah, or that creepy man or one of the other tour weirdos."

"It's probably just Calliope trying to mess with our heads," Laurie said. "No way am I falling for that."

Misti groaned. "Come on, guys, really? You don't want to know what this is about? For real?"

Laurie shook her head. "Yeah, I'm fine not knowing. No problem there."

"Really?" Misti's jaw dropped. *REALLY?*"

"Yeah."

Misti grabbed the paper. "Well, does it say anything else? Sheesh, you guys!"

She read the note and then turned the paper over in her hands. "See? There's more!" Misti thrust the paper at Laurie.

Laurie took it with two fingers, like it was a stinky dead thing. The note was written on the back of a flyer from a carnival that was set up on the edge of town, out near the SuperFoods parking lot.

"It's just a flyer." Laurie looked at it in a detached sort of way. It didn't look like it had anything to do with them. Her parents never let them go to carnivals like that, so there was no connection there. Her dad had seen the chain on one of those spinny rides break once, and the person in the seat had gone flying off and almost hit the Tilt-A-Whirl. Luckily, he'd landed on the bouncy castle and didn't end up getting that hurt, but still, Laurie's parents weren't taking any chances. Laurie shrugged and handed the flyer to Bud.

FOR TWO WEEKS ONLY
Amazing Rides! Games of Skill!
Entertainment for the whole family!
Tilt-A-Whirl—OF DEATH
Yo-Yo Ride—OF DOOM
Teacup Ride—OF WONDER
Shows four times daily, featuring:
Juanita and Her Amazing
POODLE ACROBATS!
Big Al and His Amazing Statues OF ICE!
Tiny Phil the QUICK-CHANGE ARTIST!
Rosalita and Her AMAZING VOICE!
Limited Engagement!
Follow Route 3 past the Tastee Freez,
then turn left.
DON'T MISS OUT ON THIS
AMAZING EXPERIENCE!

"I hear it's amazing," Bud deadpanned. Laurie snickered. The people who had made the flyer definitely needed a dictionary. Or at least a thesaurus. Maybe for their next birthday.

"Good grief, you guys," Misti huffed, standing up and stomping away.

Laurie and Bud watched her in silence. Then Laurie shivered. "This really freaks me out, Bud."

Bud ripped up a piece of grass. "Yeah, me too."

⁓

Misti stormed into the school without any good reason for being there. She really hoped nobody would stop her and ask what she was doing, because she didn't even have a fake answer. And in the mood she was in, she'd be liable to yell or something, and end up with detention before the school year even started.

She headed into the entryway of the school and walked slowly down the hall, checking out each and every piece of art. She'd gone through three times before she was sure she was right. That dancing frog painting had to be the screen. It was so obvious when you knew what to look for. She'd thought it was just a lousy painting, but all that mess in the background was there to hide the fact that the frog was transparent.

Misti smiled smugly to herself and hurried back down the hall to tell Bud and Laurie. She had almost made it when the voice rang out.

"Minty? Is that you?"

Misti groaned. Candy Winkle wasn't the last person she wanted to see right now, but she was close. She was maybe third from last, right after that weird clown from Misti's fifth birthday and Chuck Howard from third grade, who used to stick his pen in his ear and then suck on it.

The thought of Chuck Howard put everything in perspective. Even Candy Winkle wasn't that bad. Misti stopped and turned around. "What's up?"

Candy Winkle hurried over, followed by a thin woman in blue jeans and an I HEART MARIA TUTWEILER shirt. "Minty, what are you doing here? Are you here because of the press conference?"

Misti blinked. In a word, no. But she really wondered what Candy Winkle would say if she said yes. So she did.

Candy nodded. "I thought so, but it's not here. It's down at the courthouse. Do you know where that is?"

Misti nodded. "Thanks for telling me." She smiled at the thin lady. "Nice shirt."

Candy Winkle brightened. "Oh, do you think so? That's wonderful!" She reached out and hugged Misti, hard.

Misti tried not to look freaked out. It wasn't every

day the principal's wife hugged the stuffing out of you. Especially for just liking someone's shirt.

Candy Winkle stared at Misti with moist eyes. "Would you like one? If I gave you one, you could wear it to the press conference, wouldn't that be nice?" Candy Winkle smiled so hard her face looked like it would crack. "Wouldn't it?"

Misti nodded. "Sure, I could do that." She was always up for free school gear. She'd worn her Tuckernuck Clucker shirt so many times you could hardly see the chicken's beak anymore.

"Oh, good!" Candy Winkle grabbed the thin woman by the shoulders. "Quick, Janice, get Minty a shirt! Pronto!"

⚊⟋

Bud and Laurie were sitting on the school lawn, glumly pulling grass up by the roots, when Betty Abernathy's feet appeared directly in front of them.

Bud and Laurie looked up guiltily, trying to casually smooth over the picked-at patches.

"Bud. Laurie. I'm afraid I don't have time for our meeting today. And in fact, depending on what happens this afternoon, we may not need to meet ever again. I'll leave notes for you in your school mailboxes. Agreed?"

"Agreed," Laurie's voice sounded rough. She cleared

her throat and said it again.

Betty Abernathy nodded and eyed the turf in front of her. "Good. And now I trust you'll refrain from destroying any more school property? Thank you."

Bud and Laurie patted the ground apologetically as Miss Abernathy turned and walked away.

Laurie groaned under her breath. "What does that mean? May not need to meet ever again? Is she canceling the scavenger hunt?"

Bud shook his head. "Not the scavenger hunt. I think she's talking about Tuckernuck Hall."

What to Wear When You're Going to a
Press Conference
by Misti Pinkerton
1. I HEART MARIA TUTWEILER shirt—check.
2. Tuckernuck Cluckers hat—check.
3. What Would Maria Tutweiler Do? pin—check.
4. Shorts with CLUCKER on the butt—check.
5. MARIA TUTWEILER, OUR MOTHER CLUCKER hoodie—check.

"Oh my god, what happened to Misti?" Laurie couldn't believe her eyes. Misti looked like she'd been attacked by the gift shop and lost. It was even worse than the bedazzled sweatshirt, and that was saying something.

Bud opened his mouth and then closed it again. There was really nothing to say.

"Hey, guys, check it out!" Misti twirled around to show off her new Clucker and Maria Tutweiler gear. "Candy Winkle just *gave* it to me so I could wear it to the press conference."

"We're going to the press conference?" Bud said.

"She just assumed I was, and I wasn't going to say I wasn't, not if she was just giving all this stuff away." Misti looked at Laurie's and Bud's plain clothes and suddenly felt guilty. "I bet you could still catch her."

"That's okay," Laurie said. "That kind of stuff doesn't look half as good on me." It was actually true. Put Misti in her Clucker gear and she looked kind of cute, or at least as cute as a person could in Clucker gear. Laurie in Clucker gear just made people snicker.

"Press conference sounds good, though," Laurie said, raising her eyebrows at Bud.

"Yeah, I could go for that." There wasn't a chance

Bud was missing that press conference, but he decided to play it cool.

"Yay!" Misti crowed. "I think Candy Winkle is going to save us seats in the front row!"

EMAIL
FROM: CANDY WINKLE
TO: PRINCIPAL MARTIN WINKLE
SUBJECT: Press Conference
Angel Cakes, I had a terrific idea for something to do at the press conference today. You're going to be so happy and surprised when you see it! You'll never guess in a million years! See you there!
Kisses,
Candy
P.S. It's Minty! I dressed her in Maria Tutweiler gear, and I'm saving her a seat in the front row! That'll show that jerk LeFranco!

EMAIL
FROM: PRINCIPAL MARTIN WINKLE
TO: CANDY WINKLE
SUBJECT: Press Conference

That's great, Dumpling!

(What's minty?)

"I don't care, I'm not sitting there," Laurie hissed as Bud elbowed her in the kidneys. Misti was sitting happily in the front row, talking to Candy Winkle and waving the chicken legs on her hat. She didn't even seem to notice the weird and hostile looks she was getting from some of the other people there.

"There's an empty seat *right next to her*, Laurie," Bud said again, nudging her harder. "It would be weird for you not to sit in it."

"Drop it, Bud!" Laurie didn't have anything against sitting next to Misti. But she wasn't a front-row kind of girl, especially not at press conferences. And especially not next to someone in head-to-toe Clucker regalia. "Seriously, I think that was a bad move on Candy Winkle's part. Could she be more obvious?"

Bud shrugged. He didn't really care what Candy Winkle did, as long as he managed to divert attention away from himself. He wasn't about to sit in that empty seat.

Misti turned around in her chair and scanned the room. When she spotted Bud and Laurie, she waved her arm in the air at them. Bud nudged Laurie again. "She's signaling you."

But Laurie wasn't looking in Misti's direction. "Bud, look, it's Reginald!"

"Yeah, that makes sense," Bud said. "He's in the article, so of course he's going to be here."

"I'm going to talk to him," Laurie said, pushing past Bud and hurrying toward Reginald.

Bud watched as Laurie disappeared in the crowd and then turned back to Misti. She waved at him again. "Bud!" she stage-whispered.

Bud groaned. "Great."

Ways to Get the Janitor Who Hates You to Spill His Guts
by Laurie Madison, rising seventh grader

1. Sweet-talk him. Mention your pet peeve about liquids in inappropriate places. (DO NOT mention orange juice.)
2. Talk tough and bully him. Threaten to stick gum under desks and wear marking soles on the gym floor.
3. Beg. Cry if necessary.
4. Be perky. No one can resist perky.

"Reginald, hi!" Laurie bounced over to Reginald and smiled a big smile. He was smoking a cigarette and looking nervous. He didn't seem to be himself at all—his slicked-back hair even seemed less slick than normal.

Reginald glared at her and took a drag on his cigarette.

"So, um, that's really cool about you finding something in the school and all." Laurie bobbed merrily as she talked. She wasn't entirely sure how perky was too perky.

Reginald threw the cigarette on the ground and stomped it out. "Yeah. Excuse me now."

"NO!" Laurie stopped bobbing. She didn't know why she'd thought bobbing was perky anyway. Bobbing was irritating and dorky and had been a terrible mistake. She clutched Reginald by the arm, realized she was touching him, and then let go quickly.

"Reginald, you can tell me. Is LeFranco making you do all this? You can tell me the truth." Yeah, way to be subtle, Laurie. She felt like kicking herself.

Reginald went a shade paler. "I . . . I'm not talking to you. I have business to attend to. Now git, you."

He jerked his arm away, even though she wasn't still

holding on to it, and hurried away from her. Throwing one last panicked look over his shoulder as he went.

Bud appeared next to Laurie. "Looks like that went well."

"Shut up, Bud," Laurie muttered. "Why aren't you up there with Misti?"

"I was heading up there, but someone else grabbed that seat before I could get there. Check it out." Bud nodded his head toward the front row, where Calliope Judkin was now sitting next to Misti.

"Typical." Laurie groaned.

"Shh, children, they're starting." Some lady with a fanny pack next to Laurie gave her a nasty look.

Laurie rolled her eyes and tried to ignore her by looking up at the stage that had been set up. Reginald was standing off to the side, looking even more uncomfortable than he had five minutes ago. He wasn't making eye contact with anyone—he was just staring off into the distance. He didn't even look over when Walker LeFranco took the stage.

LeFranco smiled a big, cheesy smile at the audience and gave a silent wave. He stopped right next to a small table that had something on it. Something hidden with a large velvet drape.

"Man, he's really milking this. Is that his evidence under that cloth?" Bud whispered, getting his own dirty look from the fanny-pack lady.

"I bet it is." Laurie edged away from the fanny-pack lady.

Onstage, Walker LeFranco cleared his throat. "Thank you all for coming here today. As you know, Tuckernuck Hall employee Reginald Moore has made an amazing discovery. A discovery that solves, once and for all, the terrible murder of Alphonse Marchetti. It proves, without any doubt, that the person responsible for that murder was none other than Tuckernuck Hall founder and local eccentric Maria Tutweiler."

LeFranco's eyes gleamed as he looked around the room. Laurie suppressed a shudder. He really was enjoying this.

"Now, I know you'll have questions, and I'll let you ask Mr. Moore whatever you'd like in just a moment. But first I want to present to you—the evidence." Walker LeFranco placed a hand on top of whatever was under the drape.

"Now, Reginald is a good employee. He does his job thoroughly. So when it came time to clean out one of the little-used storerooms in Tuckernuck Hall, he did so, never anticipating what he would find."

"If he's got a skeleton under there, I'm going home," Laurie whispered.

Bud snickered.

"I'm not kidding," Laurie insisted.

The fanny-pack lady hissed at her.

"When he reported to work that day, Reginald Moore never anticipated that he would find—" Walker LeFranco whipped off the cover to reveal his evidence. "The Marchetti Bird!"

PART FIVE

DOUBLE YOUR FUN

Laurie stared at the stage. Walker LeFranco was still talking, but she couldn't hear anything, just the sound of blood pounding in her ears. She could see Misti's shocked face as she turned around in her seat to stare at Laurie and Bud. And she could see Bud's mouth hanging open as he gaped at the bird.

It was sitting there, a beautiful metal bird just like the one they'd found in the secret room. It looked exactly the same. Except the bird they'd found was still hidden. Wasn't it?

Laurie felt a hand on her arm and let herself be dragged outside into the sunlight.

"How did he get the bird?" It was Misti's voice, but Laurie hadn't even seen Misti leave her seat.

Laurie shook her head. It didn't make sense. "I don't know. Do you think he knows about the secret room?"

"He couldn't, could he?" Bud sat on the step.

"But he's got the bird! If he's got the bird, he knows about the room. Unless . . ." Misti frowned. "Are there *two* birds?"

Laurie laughed bitterly. "No, there's just the one. That's the whole point. It was one of a kind, and only Marchetti knew the secret."

"Then . . ." Misti hurried back to the doorway. "Hold on a second." She stepped quietly back inside.

Laurie and Bud exchanged a glance and then plowed back in after her.

Reginald was at the microphone. "Well, it's like I said. I was clearing the room out, and I found this bird here."

"Yes, I know." The reporter for the *Daily Herald* sounded irritated. "But where *exactly* was it? In a box? On a shelf? Where?"

Reginald glanced at Walker LeFranco. "That's it. In a box on a shelf. That's right."

Walker LeFranco stepped in front of Reginald. "Now that we've answered everything—"

"Excuse me, but I have a question."

Laurie's ears pricked up. She'd recognize Calliope's voice anywhere.

Walker LeFranco frowned. He and Calliope were neighbors, but they'd had a falling-out earlier in the year. It didn't look like they'd made up.

"Yes, Miss Judkin?" The windows almost started to frost up, his voice was so cold.

"That's a pretty bird, but can you make it work?"

Walker LeFranco glared daggers at her. "Excuse me?"

"You know, make it unfurl its wings and sing, and all the stuff the Marchetti Bird is supposed to do. If you can't make it do that, how do we know it's the real one?"

Walker LeFranco smirked at her. "It's the real one."

"So make it sing."

Walker LeFranco's smirk looked a little less smug. "Cute."

Without another word, he clapped his hands and looked over Calliope's head into the crowd. "Thank you all for coming today! I will have exclusive photos of the bird in tomorrow's paper, along with details about Tutweiler's murder plot. Thank you!"

Walker LeFranco swept the Marchetti Bird up in his arms and hustled Reginald out of the room.

Laurie stared at the door he'd gone through in shock.

She was still staring at it when Misti came running back over and grabbed her arm.

"Okay, first things first. We get back to the secret room. NOW."

"But if he found the bird, he knows! That's where he'll be going!" Bud protested.

Misti shook her head. "I don't think so. I don't think that's the same bird."

**Possible Solutions to the
Marchetti Bird Mystery
by Laurie Madison, Bud Wallace,
and Misti Pinkerton**

1. Walker LeFranco has been in the secret room and took the Marchetti Bird.
2. There are two Marchetti Birds.
3. He's got a fake.
4. We've got a fake.
5. The ghost is messing with our heads. (Contributed by Misti.)
6. Walker LeFranco is up to something. (No duh, commentary contributed by Laurie.)

"Stop!"

They were halfway to the shed when Misti skittered to a stop, forcing Bud to slam into her and knock his chin against her shoulder.

"What the heck, Misti?" Bud said, feeling around in his mouth with his tongue to make sure he still had all his teeth. He did.

"We're so stupid! This isn't going to prove anything," Misti said, rubbing her shoulder. That Bud sure had one bony chin.

"What do you mean? If the bird is there, it's not the same one. Simple." Laurie bobbed up and down on her heels. They were wasting time.

"Unless it just means that LeFranco got there before us and put it back. You know something weird's going on with that room." Misti tucked the chicken legs dangling from her hat behind her ears. "Look, this is what we do. We have to split up. You guys go check on the bird. I'll tail LeFranco and keep him and his bird in sight. If we coordinate, we'll have definite proof." Misti reached in her pocket and pulled out her hot pink phone. "I've got my baby phone. And you guys have your high-tech real phones. If we coordinate, we should be able to keep visual contact on both subjects at all times. Roger?"

Laurie nodded. She thought she knew what she had agreed to. It was hard to be sure, though, since Misti seemed to have lapsed into her own version of military talk.

"We'll meet up later," Misti said, taking off back toward the courthouse and LeFranco. "And be careful! If I'm wrong, he could be in there already!"

Misti disappeared down the road as Bud and Laurie started jogging back in the direction of the shed.

"Sure, we're the ones who are risking getting caught,"

Bud grumbled. "We're the ones risking the face-to-face in the secret room. Nice of her to wait until she was half-way down the street to point that out."

Laurie grinned at him. "You noticed that, huh? That Misti's no dummy." Then she took off at a sprint, leaving Bud in the dust.

Note to Self: Future Tips for
Tailing a Subject
by Misti Pinkerton

1. Try to keep the subject in visual range (running halfway across town and then doubling back not the best idea).

2. Try to look inconspicuous (as in, not wearing head-to-toe Clucker gear).

3. Know your subject's movements so that you can anticipate where he will go (so you don't end up scurrying around the courthouse lawn and hallways like a demented rat).

4. Have allies. (REGINALD!)

Reginald was coming down the courtyard steps when Misti spotted him and made a beeline for him.

"Oh, no. No indeed, not another one." Reginald took a step back. "I've had enough of you kids, with that girl reporter and that other liquid spiller. Just stay away from Reginald, you hear me?"

Misti tried not to be hurt. She and Laurie had only spilled one drink one time. It didn't seem fair to brand them as liquid spillers for the rest of their lives.

"I just want to talk to you!" Misti said mournfully.

"Forget it." Reginald pushed past her down the steps.

"And not even really *you*! I just wanted to know if you knew where LeFranco was going," Misti half wailed. It would've been a full wail, but she didn't want to tip LeFranco off if he was nearby.

Reginald hesitated. "That's all?"

Misti nodded. "That's all."

"No questions? Don't want to interrogate me about that bird?"

Well, yeah, sure she did. But Misti shook her head anyway. "No. Just LeFranco."

Reginald stopped and looked at her. He wasn't under any obligation to keep pesky kids away from LeFranco, especially if it got them out of his hair. And how much damage could one girl do? It's not like she had any liquids with her. And she was wearing a Clucker hat. That would really get LeFranco's goat. "He's fixing to leave. Should be in the parking lot out back still, so you better hurry if you're planning to catch him."

"Thank you!" Misti rushed forward and hugged Reginald before he knew what hit him. Then she raced off in the direction of the parking lot.

Ways to Casually Approach Subject
Without Raising Suspicion
by Misti Pinkerton

1. Ask directions. (He'll never suspect that.)
2. Don't approach, just keep in sight (pretend to be tying shoe or fixing hat).
3. Mistake him for someone else.
4. Wing it. (Cluck cluck. Ha ha.)

Misti had considered the best ways to approach LeFranco if it came to that, but she hadn't decided exactly how to do it. She was thinking the subtle approach would be best—maybe approaching him for directions, making small talk while she checked out his bird, that kind of thing. Of course, that option kind of goes out of the window when you accidentally trip over your subject's briefcase and slam into him from behind.

Misti cringed. She seemed to be lacking in basic coordination lately.

LeFranco had been kneeling down to load his draped bundle into his car trunk when Misti came wheeling around the corner, slipped on his briefcase strap, stumbled, and took a header into the small of LeFranco's back. Right where it counts.

Note stuck to the door of the shed

Kids,
Please.
A Friend

Bud crumpled the note in his fist as they crept down through the trapdoor. "That 'friend' really creeps me out." Bud attempted to make air quotes, but the crumpled paper in his hand meant his attempt was less than successful.

"Me too," Laurie confessed as they closed the trapdoor above them. "I don't think he knows about this room, though, or he would've left it there. Anybody could find a stupid note out there on the door."

Bud hoped Laurie was right. But he still had a crawling feeling on the back on his neck. They hadn't noticed anyone watching them before, but the notes proved someone sure had been. And since they hadn't realized they were being watched, Bud wasn't convinced they even knew what they should be looking for. Aside from a person standing there with binoculars or something. They'd have no problem noticing someone like that.

Calliope Judkin folded up her binoculars and stashed them in her bag. She'd followed Walker LeFranco into the hallways of the courthouse, shouting questions at him until he threatened to call the cops on her, so she'd almost lost Bud, Laurie, and Misti in the shuffle. She'd spotted them running toward the school and watched long enough to see them have some kind of animated argument and then split up.

They were definitely up to something. That Clucker gear Misti was wearing was a dead giveaway. No normal person would dress like that without a reason. No, definitely up to something. And Calliope was going to figure out what.

"Oh, wow, I'm really sorry," Misti gasped as she struggled to her feet.

"Erp," LeFranco gurgled from the pavement. He didn't seem to be in the mood to talk.

"I came around the corner, and there you were! I didn't even see you. Is that the Marchetti Bird?" Misti said, poking the drape with her toe. She wanted to peek underneath it, but she didn't want to be rude.

"Urrrgghh," LeFranco groaned, hunching over in an unflattering way.

"It is, isn't it?" Misti pushed the drape aside a little with her toe. It definitely looked like the base of the bird. She glanced at LeFranco, who was making unattractive horking noises in the back of his throat. Definitely incapacitated. She'd never have another chance like this. "Mind if I take a quick peek?"

"Narrrrr," LeFranco said, pulling himself upright. "Leave it."

"Okeydokey." Misti let the drape drop back down and smiled. "Would you excuse me? I have to make a phone call."

━━∕━━

Bud and Laurie were staring at the Marchetti Bird when Misti's call came.

They'd been sitting there, just staring at it, ever since they'd made sure the coast was clear. It was pretty boring, actually, but they didn't know what else to do. It was kind of a relief when Laurie's phone started buzzing and playing the Tuckernuck Cluckers' fight song.

"My mom programmed it," Laurie said apologetically as she flipped the phone open. "If you can figure out how to change it, for the love of god, let me know. Misti?"

Laurie listened for a few minutes. "Yeah, us too. Yeah. I've got a visual. Yeah. Yeah. Okay. Uh-huh."

Bud strained to make out what Misti's tiny voice was saying. Would it have killed Laurie to put it on speaker? Nothing like listening to half of someone else's conversation. Bud could've been a throw pillow for all the attention Laurie was paying him. But then, the throw pillows probably had a better chance of hearing what Misti was saying.

Laurie said a couple of more yeahs, a wow, a no way, and a couple of uh-huhs, and then snapped the phone shut. She grinned at Bud. "That was Misti."

Bud rolled his eyes in exasperation. "Yeah, I got that. What did she say?"

Laurie patted the Marchetti Bird. "She saw LeFranco. He's still got his bird."

Bud nodded. "So what does that mean?"

Laurie rested her hand on the Marchetti Bird's head. "One of us has got a fake. Or one of us is lying."

How to Figure Out If Your Bird Is the Real Marchetti Bird
by Laurie Madison, rising seventh grader

1. Get it to reveal all of Alphonse Marchetti's secrets. (Problem: Don't know how to do that.)
2. Get it authenticated. (Problem: By who? Marchetti Bird specialist?)
3. Make it perform tricks. (Problem: How? We're not magicians.)
4. Alternate option: Prove LeFranco's bird is fake.

"Okay, so we've verified that there are two birds," Bud said, pacing. Laurie opened her mouth. "Or at least that there are two birds *posing* as the Marchetti Bird. Because everybody knows the real bird is one of a kind," Bud hurried to finish.

Laurie shut her mouth.

"Now, thanks to Misti, we have that much to go on."
Bud couldn't help but grin. "So you really decked him?"
Bud was impressed. He'd never considered just haul-
ing off and slugging LeFranco, but in retrospect, it was
genius. He had to hand it to Misti.

"It wasn't on *purpose*," Misti said, flopping down on
the couch. "It was an accident. But that was definitely the
bird under there. Or whatever he's calling the bird. I still
think our guy is real. Can't you guys feel it?" She patted
the Marchetti Bird on the head and then tweaked its beak
affectionately. "Ours has a presence, and his is just a bird."

"Yeah, but we have to prove it," Laurie said, eyeing
the bird suspiciously. The whole morning had really
thrown her.

"So basically, our options are to expose LeFranco as
a fraud, or get our bird to do his bird things. Or both,"
Bud went on. "Preferably both."

Laurie snorted. "Oh, is that all? No problem."

Bud was going to wear out the carpet if he kept up all
that pacing stuff.

Laurie had been trying to figure out how to make the
bird work ever since Misti had called. And as far as she'd
been able to tell, there were no secret buttons, levers,
panels, keyholes, or anything anywhere on the bird they

had. It was just a solid-looking bird.

Misti squinted up at the ceiling. "How long do light-bulbs last, usually?"

"Lightbulbs? What the heck, Misti? This is serious!" Bud tried to keep his voice calm. They didn't have time to waste goofing around if they wanted to figure this thing out.

"As I see it, we've got two big problems. We can't be here trying to get the bird to work if we're trying to fig-ure out what LeFranco is up to, and we can't be figuring out what LeFranco is up to if we're in here messing with the bird."

"True." Laurie stood up. "But you're forgetting our secret weapon."

Bud blinked. They had a secret weapon? "Which is?"

Laurie smiled. "Miss Lucille."

Consulting Miss Lucille: Pros and Cons
by Laurie Madison, rising seventh grader

PROS:

1. She's about a hundred years old, so she remembers EVERYTHING.

2. She'll answer pretty much any question you ask (in a roundabout way).

3. She's pretty loopy and will probably forget
you even came by.
4. She's in the library and available.
CONS:
1. She's about a hundred years old and gets
choked up talking about dead people.
2. Everybody we need to ask about is dead.

～

Headline in the late edition of the Daily Herald

THIS BIRD WON'T SING
LeFranco reveals long-lost Marchetti Bird as evidence of murder, but is it real?

～

EMAIL
FROM: JANET DAVIS AT TUCKERNUCK HALL GIFT SHOP
TO: PRINCIPAL WINKLE
Principal Winkle,
Would you mind if we closed the gift shop early
today? The only customers we've had have been
returning their Tutweiler gear, and someone
threw an egg at the window.

Thanks,

Janet in the gift shop

EMAIL

FROM: PRINCIPAL WINKLE

TO: JANET DAVIS AT TUCKERNUCK HALL GIFT SHOP

By all means, Janet, go home. I'll let you know
whether we'll open tomorrow.

Yours,

Martin Winkle.

P.S. Did you drive today? If so, feel free to go
through the car wash and bill it to the school.
I think your egg thrower has been busy in the
parking lot, too.

Miss Lucille was building something out of Popsicle
sticks at the checkout desk in the library.

"I don't know if I'd really call Miss Lucille a secret
weapon," Bud said as they peeked through the library
window.

Laurie eyed the Popsicle sticks doubtfully. They
didn't scream "helpful source of information." Or even
"competent adult."

"She's the closest thing we've got," Laurie said. "And

she knew Maria Tutweiler. Maybe she knew Alphonse Marchetti too? It's worth a shot." Laurie took a deep breath and pulled open the library door.

Talking to Miss Lucille wasn't her favorite thing to do. No matter what she went in to talk about, it always ended up the same way—with Miss Lucille comforting her and patting her hands. The last time she'd been in there, the book she'd wanted to check out was listed as lost, and Miss Lucille had asked if Laurie was okay or if she needed to call her mother and go home.

"Here goes nothing," Laurie muttered, putting on a big happy smile and marching into the library.

EMAIL

FROM: BETTY ABERNATHY

TO: PRINCIPAL WINKLE

SUBJECT: Scavenger Hunt

Martin,

I can't help but notice the egged cars in the parking lot. And the closed gift shop. And the fact that your wife's tour group now seems to consist of one dumpy man in a hat.

Do you really think this scavenger hunt is the best use of our resources, given the uncertain future of our school? Those kids should not be coming to the school with these things going on. I, for one, am sure that Maria Tutweiler would understand if we canceled.

Yours,

Betty

EMAIL

FROM: PRINCIPAL MARTIN WINKLE

TO: BETTY ABERNATHY

SUBJECT: Not yet

Let's give it a little more time, Betty.

———

Laurie's face was getting tired. She'd been smiling for what felt like twenty years, and Miss Lucille hadn't even looked up from her stupid Popsicle sticks. The library probably did get pretty boring during the summer, but still . . . Popsicle sticks?

Laurie felt her cheek twitch. She couldn't keep it up much longer.

"Hey, Miss Lucille," she said finally.

"It's a little house for Ponch and Jon, dear. Their new habitat is nice, but they don't have a place for quiet reflection." Well, that answered that question.

"Um, yeah." Laurie glanced at Ponch and Jon, who were pushing all of their cedar chips into one corner of their cage in an attempt to make a jailbreak. Laurie hoped Miss Lucille didn't turn her back on them too often. Laurie was pretty sure just one of them could take her down.

"So that newspaper article, huh?" Laurie shifted her weight. "What do you think about that?"

Miss Lucille stuck the Popsicle-stick walls together. "What article is that, dear?"

"You know. LeFranco. Talking about Maria Tutweiler?"

Miss Lucille made a harrumphing noise. It was the most un-Miss Lucille-sounding noise Laurie had ever heard come out of her. "So you don't think it's true?"

"Of course not, it's ridiculous." Miss Lucille put the glue back down on the counter and looked at Laurie. "Anyone who knew her knows it's utter nonsense."

Laurie felt herself relax. She hadn't even realized how tense this whole thing had gotten her. "Really? That's great! I didn't think she could've murdered anybody either."

Miss Lucille gave her a strange look. "Oh, I don't know if she murdered anyone. Never said a thing to me about it, if she did. But I'm talking about that bird. The idea that Maria Tutweiler would put such a valuable bird on a shelf in a storage room? Ridiculous. She had a respect for property, you know."

Laurie's heart sank. That wasn't exactly what she'd been hoping to hear.

"So the whole bird thing is what's ridiculous?"

"Oh yes, absolutely untrue. Absolutely."

"But not the murder part?" Bud finally said. Laurie was glad he'd decided to speak up instead of just standing there like a lump of clay the whole time.

"Well, I certainly wouldn't know about that, would I?" Miss Lucille said, carefully moving the Popsicle house over to a shelf to dry.

**Disturbing Implications from Talking
to Miss Lucille
by Laurie Madison, rising seventh grader**

1. WE CAN'T SAY WHETHER MARIA TUTWEILER'S A MURDERER? CAN'T SAY? WHY CAN'T YOU SAY?
2. How many murderers does Miss Lucille know, anyway??
3. AND WHY ISN'T SHE DISTURBED BY IT?

4. Why is she more upset that LeFranco
   accused Maria Tutweiler of IMPROPERLY
   STORING THE BIRD??
5. IS MISS LUCILLE A MURDERER?
6. Get it together, Laurie. (Addendum by
   Bud Wallace.)

"Did you know Alphonse Marchetti?" Bud said, shoving Laurie to the side. She looked like she was in the early stages of a freak-out, and they didn't have time for that. They could worry about Miss Lucille's weird and twisted ethical standards later on.

"Briefly." Miss Lucille nodded. "You must remember, I was just a young girl then."

Bud nodded. "But you saw him and the bird?"

"Oh, yes, charming man. Beautiful manners, and so talented! He could do such wonderful illusions, it was amazing. And then when he disappeared . . ." Miss Lucille darted a look at Laurie.

Oh, no, Laurie thought. Here it comes. If there was one thing to bring you back from the edge of a freak-out, it was someone else losing it.

"And they said that he'd . . ." Miss Lucille grabbed Laurie's hand and started patting it. "I'm so sorry, dear, but they said he'd . . . passed on.'"

Laurie sighed and nodded. "Yes, I know. It's okay, Miss Lucille."

"You poor dear. You poor, poor dear." Miss Lucille smiled at her, misty-eyed.

"It's really okay. We really wanted to know about the bird, mostly. Did you see him use it?"

Miss Lucille brightened, but she kept rubbing Laurie's hand. It was starting to turn an interesting shade of pink.

"Oh, yes, it's an amazing bird. So beautiful, the light seems to shimmer off its body. And when it spreads its wings and sings? You never heard anything more lovely." She sighed happily.

Bud took a step closer. "Do you know how he made the Marchetti Bird work?"

"Oh, yes," Miss Lucille said, patting Laurie on the arm. Laurie flexed her hand in relief.

"You do?" she gasped.

"Of course I do. It was hardly a secret!" Miss Lucille laughed happily.

Bud and Laurie exchanged a hopeful glance. "Really? You know how it worked?"

"How to make it sing and all that? Everything?" Bud added.

"Oh, yes." Miss Lucille nodded. "Of course!"

"Could you tell us?" Laurie asked. She was almost afraid to breathe.

"Of course I can." Miss Lucille smiled at them and leaned in. "It was *magic*."

"What?" Bud's voice was flat. She had to be kidding.

"It was magic. Alphonse Marchetti was a magician, you know. He made no bones about it. Magic was what made his bird special."

"Oh, well then." Bud felt like kicking the chair, but since Miss Lucille was sitting in it, he stopped himself. "There you go, Laurie. Magic. Don't know why we didn't think of it."

"Stuff it, Bud," Laurie muttered under her breath. She smiled at Miss Lucille. "So, magic, great. Do you know how to work magic?" She figured it was worth a shot.

Miss Lucille laughed and got up. "Now, do I look like a magician?"

In a word, no.

"Well, thanks, Miss Lucille," Laurie said gloomily. It had been their best shot. And it was gone.

～

"Any luck?"

"Nope." Misti was sitting with the Marchetti Bird

on her lap. "You?"

"Nope." Laurie flopped down onto the uncomfortable couch next to her. "Miss Lucille did tell us the trick to the Marchetti Bird, though."

Misti perked up. "What is it?"

"Magic," Bud said, waggling his fingers at Misti in what he figured was a magical way.

"Oh, well that explains it, then," Misti said, petting the bird on the head and bopping it on the nose twice as she plunked it down on the coffee table. "I'm not magic."

Laurie frowned. "Good grief, Misti, it's a bird, not a drum set."

Misti shrugged her off and picked up the piece of paper. "What's this?"

Laurie waved her hand at it. "Nothing, just another message from the 'friend.' It was waiting for us."

Misti read it. "Are you guys going to answer it?"

Bud shook his head and examined the Marchetti Bird. "Nope."

Misti scowled. "You're not even *CURIOUS*?"

"It's just from some creep!" Laurie said. "Probably some jerk like Calliope!"

"Yeah, about that." Bud cleared his throat.

"What?" Laurie's voice was low and threatening. She

and Calliope didn't do well together.

Bud perched on the chair. "Okay, this is how I see things. Tell me if I'm wrong."

Laurie and Misti exchanged a doubtful glance. This didn't sound good.

"We need to figure out the bird, right?" Bud started.

"No duh, Bud, save us the speech. You've said this all before. We know. We need to figure out the bird and figure out LeFranco and we suck at both. Now cut to the chase."

"We need help," Bud said.

"No duh." If Laurie hadn't been in a secret room closed up for a gazillion years, she would've thrown a tasseled pillow at him. But you just can't chuck pillows that have been closed up in a secret room, no matter how much you want to.

"I think I know where we can get it. Help, I mean." Bud had that shifty-eyed look on his face. Laurie didn't like it.

"The friend from the note?" Misti said cautiously.

Bud shook his head. "No. Not there."

"You'd better not be saying what I think you're saying," Laurie warned.

"Laurie, she lives *right next door* to LeFranco. She

obviously doesn't like him. She'd be glad to help! Plus, you can tell from her questions today—she's done research too!"

Misti looked from Bud to Laurie. She'd never seen Laurie look so ticked off. She looked like she might accidentally set the room on fire with her laser-beam eyes.

"Who are we talking about here?"

"Calliope," Laurie growled.

Reasons Calliope Judkin Can Never Ever Help Us
by Laurie Madison, rising seventh grader

1. She's a menace.
2. She has EVERYTHING—good grades, cuteness, first place on everything in the world. Why give her this, too?
3. She can't be trusted with a secret—she's a REPORTER, for goodness' sake.
4. She almost RUINED the treasure hunt last year. She almost got us ARRESTED.
5. ETC. (There is not enough paper in the world to list them all.)

"I'm leaving it up to Laurie," Misti said. "But she does seem a wee bit pushy in class."

"Ha! Wee bit?" Laurie ranted. She had been arguing for what felt like a million years. And the worst part was, at the edges of her mind, she was afraid Bud might have a point. "Bud, look, here's the thing. Even if she doesn't mess everything up, she'll know about the room! Do you want her to know about the room?"

"Lightbulbs," Misti said quietly.

"Of course not, but I don't see that we have any options! Do you?" Bud really didn't get the whole thing Laurie had with Calliope. Sure, she was irritating, but that was mostly because Calliope had a thing for Bud. It wasn't his fault that she had a crush, so he tried to be nice to the poor kid.

"The lightbulbs," Misti said again.

"Misti, what the heck?" Bud said. She'd been ranting about the stupid lightbulbs all day.

"They don't change themselves," Misti said. "Do you really think that lightbulbs that someone put in decades ago would still work? I don't."

They all stared at the lightbulbs in the fixtures overhead. "Oh, crud," Bud said.

"We won't be able to keep this secret forever," Misti

said. "Not if the lightbulbs are changing."

Laurie sat down again. "Do ghosts change lightbulbs, Misti?"

Misti looked doubtful. "I don't know if they do."

Sad Truths About the Secret Room
by Laurie Madison, rising seventh grader

1. If four of us are going in and out, one of us is eventually going to get caught.
2. If four of us know about it, eventually one of us is going to tell someone.
3. If one of us tells someone, that person is eventually going to tell someone.
4. Once that happens, the entire seventh grade is going to end up camped out in Maria Tutweiler's secret room.
5. Once someone is caught, the secret is out. Once someone tells, the secret is out.
6. It's probably already too late to stop it, whether we tell Calliope or not.

Bud, Laurie, and Misti closed the trapdoor and peered out of the shed to make sure the coast was clear.

"Just think about it, Laurie. Calliope likes me. I think

she'd go for it. Don't you want to take LeFranco down?"

Laurie nodded slowly. Bud smiled and made a dash across the yard.

Misti bumped Laurie sympathetically. "It won't be that bad, maybe," she said. "But it's up to you."

"Maybe you're right." Laurie gave her a weak grin. "Now get home, before your mom decides to bedazzle your whole wardrobe."

Misti gasped and hurried out of the shed without checking.

Laurie giggled. That had just been a joke, but apparently the threat of bedazzlement was a bigger risk than she'd realized.

She peered out into the empty yard and set her jaw. She knew what she had to do.

Text message from Laurie Madison to Bud Wallace

Okay, fine, call Calliope. She's in.

EMAIL
FROM: BUD WALLACE
TO: CALLIOPE JUDKIN

SUBJECT: Get together?

Hey, Calliope,

What do you say we get together tomorrow? I have some stuff I'd like to talk to you about.

Your friend,

Bud Wallace

EMAIL

FROM: CALLIOPE JUDKIN

TO: BUD WALLACE

SUBJECT: HAI

Stop dreaming, Bud. I'm not going out with you.

EMAIL

FROM: BUD WALLACE

TO: CALLIOPE JUDKIN

SUBJECT: WHAT?

You're the one who's dreaming, Calliope! I'm not asking you out on a DATE. I just want to talk to you! Just meet me outside the school at one o'clock. And don't worry. Laurie Madison and MIsti Pinkerton will be there if you feel like you need a CHAPERONE.

Bud

EMAIL
FROM: CALLIOPE JUDKIN
TO: BUD WALLACE
SUBJECT: No promises
I'll take it under advisement.

Note to Self
by Calliope Judkin
HIGHLY SUSPICIOUS ACTIVITY—Bud Wallace/Laurie Madison/Misti Pinkerton want to meet? Very suspicious. Could be a setup. Research necessary.
BRING BACKUP.

Note stuck to door of shed

Okay, "Friend."
Name the time and place.
— One of the kids

PART SIX

TUCKERNUCK UNDERCOVER

Laurie crept down the stairs and sat on the bottom step in her entryway. She could hear her parents in the other room. Or sort of hear them. She'd caught the words "Tuckernuck," "bird," and "Tutweiler," so she knew they were talking about the murder. But beyond that, it was hard to say.

Laurie hadn't managed to piece together much more when she heard her brother creep down the stairs after her. Jack sat down next to her. "What are we listening to?"

"Shh!" Laurie hissed. She was supposed to be asleep, but she didn't think she needed to worry about him busting her, since Jack was supposed to be asleep too. "They're talking about the newspaper articles." She hesitated. "I think."

"Then come on," Jack whispered, silently getting up and creeping across the hall. "Dining room's better for eavesdropping. There's a vent."

Laurie hurried across the hall to where Jack was kneeling next to the vent between the living room and the dining room. "Listen," he mouthed.

Laurie nodded. Her parents' voices were much clearer here. She couldn't believe she was just now finding that out.

"Fine, let's say she did it. She's a terrible person. But even if she is a murderer, that won't shut the school, will it?" Mrs. Madison's voice sounded strained. "It seems so ridiculous!"

"Well, ridiculous or not, I talked to Trinity Harbaugh's father at the grocery store and he's sending her to Savannah Heights next year. And he said Linda and Ray Silver are doing the same thing with Sam."

"That's just crazy!"

Laurie could hear her dad pacing. "Is it? These people . . . you saw how quick they were to hop on the Tuckernuck bandwagon when Laurie found the treasure. And now they're just as quick to believe the worst."

Laurie stared at her brother in horror. Sam Silver and Trinity Harbaugh? If kids dropped out of the school, it wouldn't matter how much LeFranco was lying. He'd win anyway.

Jack shook his head, his mouth set in a grim line. "Sorry, kiddo," he said, punching her lightly on the shoulder.

Laurie shook her head violently. "It's not over!" she hissed.

Jack gave her a long, solemn look. And then he forced

himself to smile. "Sure. You're right. It's not over till it's over."

But he didn't sound like he believed it. And Laurie wasn't sure she believed it herself.

~

Bud was in the basement, waging a dinosaur war against his dad's model revolutionary troops, when he heard his dad call him. Sure, he was probably getting a little old for plastic dinosaur battles, but he'd just gotten the dinosaurs back not long ago, and he was constantly amazed at how much they would've changed the Revolutionary War.

"Bud, Flora's leaving! Come say good-bye!"

Bud put his triceratops in the boat crossing the Delaware and started up the stairs.

"BUD!" his dad called again.

Bud opened his mouth to yell back that he was coming when Miss Downey's voice stopped him.

"That's okay, Wally, let him stay down there."

Bud hesitated. If she didn't care if he said good-bye, he sure wasn't going to bother. But he didn't want to tick his dad off either.

"No, he should—"

"I meant to mention, Wally. Principal Winkle has

called a special meeting tomorrow for some of the teachers." Flora Downey sounded like she was measuring every word. It gave Bud a cold feeling down his back.

"What about? Is it serious?"

"It could be. It's about the charges in the paper. Apparently a lot of parents are taking it seriously. Betty Abernathy told me that the whole future of the school is in doubt."

"What, again? This is ridiculous!" Bud's dad sounded confused. "Over a couple of articles? It's only been a couple of days!"

"Apparently a couple of days is all it takes for the public to turn on you. And Walker LeFranco has them eating out of his hand. That Marchetti Bird—it's silenced most of the doubters. Once he gets it to work, the whole town will be in his pocket."

"Well, maybe that won't happen." Bud's dad sounded doubtful.

Miss Downey snorted.

Bud cringed. Teachers shouldn't snort. She might as well just fart and burp the alphabet and be done with it. "Wally, he has the Marchetti Bird. It's only a matter of time before he gets it to sing, and then it'll be all over. That bird is legendary."

"Well, that's just insane. Until it does, I refuse to worry about it. I've wasted too much time worrying about things that weren't important, and I just made Bud's life miserable. I refuse to do it again." The door to the basement jerked open. "BU— Oh! Bud, there you are. Flora is heading home."

Bud gave his dad a weak smile and trooped the rest of the way up the stairs.

Note from Calliope Judkin to her backup

You know the drill. Stay out of sight. I'll be meeting with the three Lame-a-teers. First sign of trouble, you make your move.
BUT NO SOONER.

Calliope

EMAIL

FROM: CANDY WINKLE

TO: PRINCIPAL MARTIN WINKLE

SUBJECT: Tours

Bad news, Lovebug.

Everyone signed up for the tour has canceled

today. And I mean everyone, even our tour-
obsessed friend.

I'll hang around the office in case we have any
walkups, but it seems doubtful. Some of the
messages on the machine were quite abusive.

Kisses,

Candy

EMAIL

FROM: PRINCIPAL MARTIN WINKLE

TO: CANDY WINKLE

SUBJECT: Tours

Just stay put, Tweety Bird. I've got that meeting
with the teachers this afternoon, but we can
both head out after that.

Love,

Your Snoopy Dog

EMAIL

FROM: BUD WALLACE

TO: LAURIE MADISON AND MISTI PINKERTON

SUBJECT: Calliope

So I emailed Calliope, and we're all set to meet
later today. Trust me, she'll be cool. This will be

a piece of cake.

See you later,

Bud

"Forget it." Calliope folded her arms. "I'm not agreeing to anything."

"Come on, Calliope!" Bud tried not to look at Laurie and Misti. This whole Calliope thing was his idea, and if it tanked, he'd look like an idiot.

Calliope rolled her eyes at him. "One—you want me to join your little gang or whatever, but you're not willing to give details until I agree and swear myself to secrecy, which as a reporter, is a *STUPID* thing to do. Two—you won't even tell me what it's about, except that you want to take LeFranco down, and excuse me, I am doing a fine job of that on my own." She sighed. "Look, guys, I can see why you'd need my help, okay? For whatever little thing you're doing. But here's the big question. Why in the world would I need you?"

Misti tapped Bud on the shoulder. "Huddle." She nodded her head at Calliope. "Excuse us for a second."

Misti dragged Bud and Laurie a few feet away while Calliope waited, impatiently tapping her foot.

"This isn't going to work, Bud. We can't say, 'Hey, join

us for this secret thing, so we can do this other secret thing that we can't tell you about until you agree, but seriously, it's really cool.' *NO ONE* would agree to that."

Laurie nodded. "There's only one way to do this. She has to see the secret room."

"NO!" Bud paled visibly. "What if she says forget it and then spills the beans? We can't do that! She can't see it until she agrees!" Bud had lost all faith in his ability to charm Calliope. Apparently all those years of blowing her off had caught up with him.

Laurie smirked. "There's a way. I came prepared." She reached into her backpack and pulled out a red bandanna, which she flipped around in circles until it was blindfold shaped.

Bud nodded in agreement. "Nice."

"Okay, Calliope, turn around," Laurie said, advancing with the bandanna in her hand. "You want to see what we're talking about? We have to take precautions."

Calliope looked at the bandanna in disgust. "You have got to be kidding me."

"No joke, Calliope. This is big. You'll understand when you see it. But first, blindfold."

Calliope hesitated. Laurie could almost see her antennae twitching. Laurie decided to go in for the kill.

"Wear the blindfold, don't wear the blindfold, it doesn't matter to me, Calliope. But know this—if you don't put it on, you'll *NEVER* know what the secret is."

Calliope cracked. The thought of never finding out what they were up to was just too much for her. "Fine, blindfold. Whatever. You guys are majorly weird, though, okay? I've *SEEN* you. You're not normal."

She turned around so Laurie could tie the blindfold, but then stopped her. "Hold on, I've got to call off the backup."

"What?" Bud felt betrayed. She had backup? What kind of kid thinks to bring backup?

"It's okay, Montana! You're relieved of duty! Just go home! I'll meet you there later!" Calliope yelled at the bushes.

"What?" A tiny girl who looked like a miniature Calliope popped up from the middle of a lilac bush. "You don't need backup?"

"My sister, Montana. She's eight," Calliope said, like it explained everything. "It's fine, I'll meet you back home!" she yelled back at Montana.

"Are you sure?" Montana looked ticked off.

Bud couldn't believe it. He'd had no idea there was anyone inside that lilac bush. It looked just like all the other lilac bushes. He couldn't believe he'd been so easy to fool.

"I'm sure! Go home!" Calliope yelled with an edge in her voice. Bud hoped this wouldn't turn into one of those sibling screaming matches he'd heard about.

Montana Judkin looked disappointed. "Okay, fine. But my rate hasn't changed! You still owe me the five dollars!" Montana hitched up her overall-shorts strap and stomped out of the lilac bush and down the street.

Bud stared at Calliope, his mouth still hanging open. He'd had no idea of the depths she was willing to sink to.

Calliope looked vaguely guilty. "What? How was I supposed to know what you guys were going to pull? It's good to have backup," Calliope grumbled. "Now hurry up with the blindfold."

"Mouth, Bud," Laurie said as she tied the blindfold around Calliope's head. "Close it?"

Bud closed his mouth. He wasn't sure how he felt about this new side of Calliope, what with her secret backup plans and all, but it was too late to back out now. He took Calliope by the arm, and then the three of them led her carefully across the school yard toward the shed.

BILL

TO: CALLIOPE JUDKIN

FROM: MONTANA JUDKIN

SERVICES RENDERED

Spying on subjects *LAURIE MADISON,* *BUD WALLACE, MISTI PINKERTON*:	$2.50
Providing backup for secret meeting:	$2.50
TOTAL DUE:	$5.00

EMAIL

FROM: CANDY WINKLE

TO: PRINCIPAL MARTIN WINKLE

SUBJECT: Your Kids

Sweetie, I don't mean to disturb you before your meeting, but those kids of yours are really strange. They seem to be playing some blindfolding game out back? Either that or they just kidnapped another student. I just thought you should be aware.

Kisses,

Candy

EMAIL

FROM: PRINCIPAL MARTIN WINKLE

TO: CANDY WINKLE

SUBJECT: Kidnapping

Thanks, Snuggle Bunny,

Now if any of the kids turn up kidnapped, we

have a lead!

You're the best.

Love,

Your Snickerdoodle

Bud positioned Calliope in the middle of the room, facing the sofa, while Misti carefully took the Marchetti Bird out of its cabinet and placed it in the middle of the coffee table. They'd taken to putting everything back exactly the way they'd found it when they left the room, mostly because the shock of finding things mysteriously put away every day was pretty unpleasant.

On the count of three, Laurie whipped the blindfold off of Calliope's head, only briefly getting it caught on her ear.

Calliope's eyes widened as she looked around the room, and then got even wider when she saw the bird. Then she clenched her jaw, folded her arms, and turned to Bud. "What is this place?"

"Secret room."

"Okay, I'm in."

REQUEST FOR SERVICES
FROM: Calliope Judkin
TO: Montana Judkin
CLIENT: CALLIOPE JUDKIN
  BE ON CALL FOR: Spying, eavesdropping, tailing, other duties as assigned.

RATE: $2.50 per assignment

(APPROVE) DISAPPROVE

Approved by: MONTANA JUDKIN

Plan of Attack
by Calliope Judkin

Tailing LeFranco: Montana

On Bird: Misti, Laurie

On Research: Calliope, Bud

RECONVENE AT FIFTEEN HUNDRED HOURS

Note from Misti Pinkerton to Laurie Madison

Fifteen hundred hours means three o'clock, right?

Note from Laurie Madison to Misti Pinkerton

I think so. That's what I'm going with, anyway.

"So Montana's not going to know anything about the secret room, right?" Laurie wanted to be absolutely clear on that point. It was bad enough having Calliope in there without having it turn into an eight-year-old's clubhouse.

"Geez, no. You think I want her knowing about this?" Calliope scoffed. "Trust me, she's strictly a contract employee."

"Good."

Calliope looked around the room. "Now, you guys have gone through all this stuff? All these notebooks and things?"

Laurie cringed. "Well, some of them. Not all. There's not much there, though. It's mostly budget stuff, it looks like. And the papers look like they belonged to Maria Tutweiler's dad." She'd had a little time for exploring when she wasn't tearing her hair out over the Marchetti Bird.

"Plus it's cursive." Misti shrugged.

"Okay, we can start there. Montana's on LeFranco now, so if he leaves his house, we'll know his movements. We should have this all wrapped up in no time."

Text message from Montana Judkin to Calliope Judkin

> Lizard Lips is on the move. He just left the house and is messing with the keys to that ugly green station wagon out front.

Text message from Calliope Judkin to Montana Judkin

> Thanks. Roger that.

Text message from Calliope Judkin to Montana Judkin

> Out of curiosity, why Lizard Lips?

Text message from Montana Judkin to Calliope Judkin

> Seriously? Don't you think he looks like Billy Prescott's lizard, Maury? They could be twins.
>
> Attachment: MaurytheLizard.jpg

Text message from Calliope Judkin to Montana Judkin

> Fine, they're twins, now GO! Follow him!

~

Headline in the Morning News *late edition*

> # EVIDENCE OVERWHELMING: TUTWEILER IMPLICATED IN VILE MURDER
> ## Police Chief Skip Burkiss: Marchetti Investigation May Be Reopened

Channel 7 online news teaser

Tonight on News 7—HIDDEN DANGERS IN YOUR COMMUNITY! Does going to a school founded by a murderer put your child at risk? The answer may surprise you. Investigative report tonight at 10.

Headline in the Daily Herald *late edition*

> # MARCHETTI EVIDENCE REMAINS UNCONFIRMED
> ## Famed Marchetti Bird reported found, but experts refused access, demonstration not forthcoming.

—∕—

Bud looked up from the notebook he'd been going through. It was a pretty detailed account of the expenses for the school the first year it was open, but no matter how you sliced it, there was no chance the school's chalk budget was going to be exciting. "Anything?" he said to Calliope.

"Not yet," Calliope said without looking up. "We'll find something."

"Laurie said these are just budget ledgers. I don't think Maria Tutweiler would confess to murder in the middle of the cafeteria expense account."

"You never know, Bud. It pays to be thorough," Calliope said testily.

Bud shoved the ledger away and got up. "I'm done with mine. I'm going to head out and see what else I can dig up. It's okay if we split up, right?"

Calliope hesitated and then closed her ledger. "You know, we probably don't have time to be too thorough." Calliope grabbed her bag. "Get your stuff. We need to forget about researching Maria Tutweiler. We need to be researching LeFranco."

Bud did a mental fist pump. Now she was talking.

—∕—

Text message from Montana Judkin to Calliope Judkin

> Lizard Lips is at the Morning News building. He's been there FOREVER. As of right now, you're covering expenses. Because this stakeout required a pack of mini donuts and a large soda.

Text message from Calliope Judkin to Montana Judkin

> Fine. Expenses approved.

Text message from Montana Judkin to Calliope Judkin

> Great! And did I say one pack of mini donuts?
> I meant to say two.

Misti craned her head and peered up at the Marchetti Bird's base. Laurie had been holding it up for what felt like an hour, but was probably closer to five minutes.

"Anything?" Laurie said finally. Her arms were getting tired. How much was there for Misti to look at, anyway?

"Nothing," Misti said. "You can put it down."

They'd gone at the Marchetti Bird with a magnifying glass and a flashlight, but they still couldn't see any sign that the thing actually could move, let alone figure out how to make it work.

Laurie sighed and put the huge bird back on the table. "Maybe there's nothing to see. Maybe this isn't the real bird."

Misti shook her head and patted the Marchetti Bird on its sides, like she was frisking it for contraband. "It's the real bird. I can feel it."

Text message from Montana Judkin to Calliope Judkin

BOOORING! Lizard Lips went to the bank. I continued the tail inside and acted like I was trying to open a Christmas Club account. He took out some money, but I couldn't see how much.

I had to pretend I was with Mrs. Baker from down the street (you know, the lady with the thousand kids?) so he couldn't ID me.
He was totally fooled.

Text message from Montana Judkin to Calliope Judkin

> P.S. I think the stress from this assignment might require some more mini donuts. And maybe a burger and large fries. Have to keep my strength up.

—⁓—

"Hey, Ron," Calliope said as she pushed open the door to the *Daily Herald* offices.

"Are we allowed to be here?" Bud whispered, walking nervously into the room. It wasn't exactly what he'd expected from a newspaper office, but still, there were actual reporters at actual desks. It wasn't a place Bud felt comfortable crashing.

"Oh, sure, they know me," Calliope said. She marched up to the man at the closest desk. "So, Ron, background on the LeFrancos. Father *and* son. Do you guys have that?"

Ron gave a huge fakey sigh and glared at Calliope. "Again, Calliope? You know I'm not supposed to give you that stuff anymore."

"Okay then," Bud said, making tracks back toward the door. Didn't have to tell him twice. "Too bad."

Calliope just grinned. "No problem, Ron, we'll just head back to the archives then. Come on, Bud."

Ron picked up a folder on his desk and swatted Calliope with it. "Can't even mess with you anymore. Here you go—I figured you'd be by."

Calliope smiled and took the folder. "Thanks, Ron. See you soon!"

She turned and trotted out.

"Is he supposed to do that?" Bud said, hurrying after her. "Isn't that illegal or something?"

"Just keep your trap shut, Bud, and nobody will find out," Calliope said, her face serious. Then she punched Bud in the shoulder and smiled. "No, seriously, this is just pulled news clips. Anybody could get it. Ron just saved us some time. He can be our contact when we bring LeFranco down. We give him the exclusive, nobody will care." Calliope stopped and poked Bud in the chest. "Exclusive, cowritten by *me*, got it?"

"Uh, okay," Bud said, hurrying to keep up with Calliope. He had a feeling that he was going to have a lot of keeping up to do.

Text message from Montana Judkin to Calliope Judkin

Mr. Excitement is at the hardware store. Talking hardware blah blah with the hardware guys. My brain can *only take so much hardware talk before it rebels, so I had to excuse myself to have a candy bar or two. Besides, I didn't want to risk having him spot me, endanger the mission, etc., etc. Don't worry, I'm saving my receipts.*

~~

"Are you sure your mom won't mind us using her computer?" Laurie said, perching on the embroidered computer stool nervously. She'd never seen so much craftwork in her entire life. There wasn't an inch of space in the room that hadn't been embroidered, latch hooked, cross-stitched, bedazzled, stenciled, or decoupaged.

"It's fine, we just need to hurry," Misti said, logging on.

"So we'll be done before she needs to use it?" Laurie asked.

"So we'll be done before she figures out how to redesign our outfits." Misti tapped furiously on the computer keyboard.

Laurie took a deep breath. It was time to say something. After all, you can only see your friend attacked by sequins for so long before you have to try to save them. "Is this a . . . new thing? I don't remember her being so . . . crafty before."

Misti nodded without stopping her typing. "It's a new thing. It'll pass. We just have to wait it out."

Laurie nodded. Hopefully it would pass before her mom spotted them.

Misti finished typing. "Okay, check it out. Here's some stuff on the bird."

Laurie leaned in to look, just as a door slammed somewhere else in the house.

Misti stiffened. "Oh, boy. It's my mom." Her eyes widened in horror.

Misti's mom's voice came from somewhere down the hall. "Misti? Is your little friend still here? I have the cutest idea!"

⌒

"What the—" Bud gasped. "What happened to you?"

Laurie shot him a nasty look. "Shut up, Bud." Laurie reached up and touched the spangled headband she was wearing. She knew she should've tried to get it off earlier, but Misti's mom had done a really thorough job of braiding it into her hair. It was blue but otherwise perfectly matched the green one on Misti's head.

"You look like you escaped from a music video from the eighties." Bud snickered.

"Stuff it." Laurie reached up and pulled her headband

out of her hair. A clump of hair came out with it, but Laurie figured it was a necessary sacrifice.

"Did you at least find anything out about the bird? Or was it just makeover time?" Bud smirked, leaning over to grab the headband. She snatched it away and stuffed it into her pocket, making it look like her shorts were exploding into blue spangly sparkles on one side. No matter what Bud said, she didn't want to lose it just yet. It hadn't been a terrible look for her.

"No, that's the worst part," Misti said, sitting down next to the Marchetti Bird and tapping it on its tail. "We found a thousand ways it *doesn't* work. And we found a bunch of people who tried to make their own Marchetti Birds but couldn't."

"In a nutshell, nobody knows how it works, and nobody's made one since. It's a mystery. The end." Laurie shook her head. She felt like she had glitter in her ears. It was like she'd been attacked by a horde of fairies. It gave her new respect for Misti—she must have to be on guard every second.

Calliope sat down on the footstool. "Great. So we're nowhere on the bird front. Terrific, guys."

Laurie didn't know if Calliope was trying to sound snarky or if she just couldn't help it, but either way Laurie didn't appreciate it. "Okay, Calliope, what did you come up with. Anything?"

"Of course," Calliope said.

"No," Bud said at the same time.

They exchanged a look.

"Well, okay, not much," Calliope admitted. "We got some basic background on the LeFrancos, though. The feud between the LeFrancos and Maria Tutweiler had been going on for a while, but it seems to have heated up around the time Marchetti disappeared. But we couldn't find out why they hated each other. It didn't say anything specific in the news clips."

Misti sighed. "Well, that's frustrating." She bopped the bird on the head, petted its tail feathers, and tweaked its beak.

"No kidding," Calliope said. "We're not totally out of luck, though. Montana's been tailing LeFranco all day. She's sure to have turned up some dirt."

Text message from Montana Judkin to Calliope Judkin

Hate LeFranco. Got nothing. He went home. I'm out front staring at his boring house. Please fire me.

"So she's got nothing?" Bud sat down hard on the uncomfortable couch, his weight making Misti bob up like an apple in a bucket.

"Less than nothing." Calliope said, clicking off her cell phone. "She didn't see anything, and it sounds to me like her next stakeout is going to be in the downstairs bathroom. She ate a lot of candy today," Calliope explained when Laurie looked grossed out.

"I *GOT* it," Laurie said. "Geez, TMI, okay?"

"It's not *my* fault she's a pig! She said LeFranco went to the bank and withdrew money, which could be something. And he went to the hardware store, which could be something, except she used that opportunity to go to the 7-Eleven next door, so we don't know what he bought."

"Great." Bud groaned.

"We can't just give up!" Misti said, nervously patting the Marchetti Bird on the head repeatedly. Pat pat pat pat, pet pet pet. It was getting on Bud's nerves. He bit his tongue, though, and didn't say anything. The last thing they needed to do now was fight.

"Of course we're not going to give up," Bud said, trying to stay patient. "I didn't say that."

"Misti's right," Laurie said. "There's got to be

something we're overlooking."

Misti nodded and resumed her patting and petting. Pet pet, pat pat, bop.

Bud gritted his teeth. He felt like grabbing her hands. "So what? Talk to Miss Lucille again? See what LeFranco does next? It feels like we're always a step behind him."

"I don't want to wait," Misti said. Pat pat pat, pet pet pet. Bop.

"MISTI, CUT IT OUT!" Bud couldn't take it anymore.

Bop. Misti stopped after that last bop and looked up at him. "What? Bud, what are you—"

She never finished the sentence, though. Because a strange low tone was coming from the middle of the table.

Calliope's eyes widened. "Misti, what did you *DO?*"

Misti stared at the bird in horror. "I didn't do anything! I just petted it!"

The tone grew in intensity until it seemed like it filled the whole room. And then, slowly, the Marchetti Bird began to vibrate.

And then, before anyone realized exactly what was happening, the Marchetti Bird spread its wings and began to sing.

PART SEVEN

THE MARCHETTI
BIRD REVEALS ALL

EMAIL

FROM: PRINCIPAL MARTIN WINKLE

TO: CANDY WINKLE

SUBJECT: Meeting

Hi, Sunshine,

The meeting is over, and I'm afraid Tuckernuck
Hall Intermediate School may be too. The
teachers have all been hearing the same sort of
things I am, and that's not encouraging. I may
have to turn in my Clucker hat for good.

Kisses,

Your Sugar Dumpling

P.S. Any sign of our kidnappee?

EMAIL

FROM: CANDY WINKLE

TO: PRINCIPAL MARTIN WINKLE

SUBJECT: False alarm!

Hi, Shortcake,

I saw the kidnapped girl again, so I think I was
either mistaken about the kidnapping or she
escaped unharmed. One question, though—is
there something special about that shed out

back? The kids seem to be spending a lot of time
there. It could be a safety hazard.
I'm sorry about your meeting. We'll stop by
Krispy Kreme on the way home. You always feel
better when you've had a doughnut.
Kisses,
Candy

—

Bud stared at Misti like she'd sprouted a couple of extra
heads and a set of wings. "Did you hit a secret button or
what?"

Misti waved him off. "Quiet, Bud! It's singing!"

The Marchetti Bird finished its song and then slowly
folded its wings back against its body. And when it
stopped moving, a small hidden drawer in the base of
the statue popped open.

Misti gasped. Bud and Laurie exchanged an excited
look, crowded forward, and peered inside. There, in
the bottom of the shallow drawer, was a faded and
ancient envelope addressed in flowing and elaborate
script.

To my friends.

"Is that . . . ," Bud started.

Laurie nodded. "All the secrets of his life."

My Dear Friend,

And I feel I must call you friend if my marvelous bird has chosen to reveal all her secrets to you. She is a jealous guardian, and would not take you into her confidence lightly.

If everything has gone according to plan, no one has seen me alive since the night of August 17. If all has gone according to plan, I disappeared midperformance, leaving no sign of my whereabouts, save for a gruesome crime scene splashed with copious amounts of blood.

But of course my lovely bird knew that I had not met my demise on that warm summer evening. I had to share with her the truth

about my murder. And now she can share that
truth with you.

Laurie stopped reading and looked at the others. "It's from Alphonse Marchetti," she breathed. "It's really him."

"Let me guess—it ends there, right? Maybe with a big bloodstain on it or something?" Bud said. It would be just his luck to find a letter that didn't tell them anything.

Laurie grinned. "Nope, we're good. It keeps going," she said, waving the letter happily before starting to read again.

In recent weeks, I have found myself in
an increasingly difficult position. Leroy
"Bull" Stratton, the head of the city's
organized crime syndicate, saw my performance
at the Majestic and became convinced that
my illusions could help him with his illicit

activities. He offered me a position within his organization, and I refused. However, I came to understand that his offer was less than optional, and my refusal angered him and his cohorts. Numerous attempts have been made on my life. I have shared my knowledge with local police, but, sadly, that has not ensured my safety. It has only made me a canker that Stratton and his followers are determined to cut out. There was only one way I could ensure my future well-being.

With the help of my dear friend Maria Tutweiler, I faked my disappearance and death. When I disappeared from the Celestial's stage on the evening of August 17, I quickly made my way backstage and into the alley, where Maria was waiting with her car. I was gone before the audience

was aware anything was amiss. Maria and I

had previously secured a large quantity of blood

from a butcher who I believe can be trusted.

After my escape from the theater, Maria

whisked me away to her secret quarters, and

with the help of Officer Arthur Martin

of the local police force, she made use of the

blood, staging a horrific scene in my home. I

can only pray their efforts will be convincing.

I must now say good-bye to my life

as Alphonse Marchetti, magician and

illusionist. With the help of Officer

Martin, I have secured an alternate identity

and will begin a new life. Alphonse

Marchetti will never walk out of this room.

It is with deep regret that I leave him behind,

*and with him, my most treasured friend, the
Marchetti Bird. Care for her well, and
with luck, someday I may return.*

Yours eternally,

Alphonse Marchetti

"Do you think he ever returned?" Misti sighed, patting the Marchetti Bird tentatively once on the head. She was afraid to pat it more than that—she didn't want to accidentally set off its self-destruct mode or something.

"Obviously he didn't. If he did, we wouldn't have found any of this. And it's not like he's going to return now—that was all, what, seventy or eighty years ago?" Calliope looked at the bird with a gleam in her eye. "Man, this is going to be an incredible scoop."

Laurie shook her head. "Oh, no, you don't. You don't breathe a *word* of this. Not until we *all* decide what we're going to do." She held the papers to her chest. She was prepared to stuff them down her shirt if she had to.

"She's right," Bud said quietly. "No one says a thing. Not yet. Agreed?"

Calliope looked from Misti and the bird to Bud and then to Laurie. "Fine. Agreed," she said. But the gleam didn't leave her eyes. If Calliope said she agreed, Laurie had to believe her, but she still had a bad feeling about it in the pit of her stomach.

Laurie looked at the papers in her hand. "There's more here. It's not just the letter. There's a thing signed by Officer Martin, and some more papers, and . . . this."

"What is it?" Misti leaned in to look.

"It's a photo. Of . . . I don't know, actually. A bunch of guys." Laurie passed the photo to Calliope and handed the rest of the papers to Misti.

"Well, I recognize this man," Calliope said, pointing at the photo.

Bud took the photo and looked closely at it. "It's not Marchetti."

Calliope smirked. "Nope. It's Wayne LeFranco. Walker LeFranco's dad."

⤳

Note left on door of shed

> *Tomorrow morning. 11 a.m.*
> *—A Friend*

Headline on Daily Herald *website*

PROTESTS PLANNED FOR TOMORROW AT TUCKERNUCK HALL
Anger grows at allegations of criminal activities of Founder Maria Tutweiler

---

Headline on Morning News *website*

PETITION TO CLOSE TUCKERNUCK HALL GAINING MOMENTUM
Click here to sign online petition.

EMAIL

FROM: BETTY ABERNATHY

TO: PRINCIPAL MARTIN WINKLE

SUBJECT: WELL?

Martin,

Things are getting ugly. Have you reconsidered about the scavenger hunt?

Thanks,

Betty

EMAIL

FROM: PRINCIPAL MARTIN WINKLE

TO: BETTY ABERNATHY

SUBJECT: YOU WIN.

Betty,

You're right—we should put it on hold for now.
I'm not going to cancel it outright, but the kids
don't need to be hanging around the school in
this atmosphere.

We'll tell them at the meeting tomorrow.

Thanks,

Martin

Text message from Montana Judkin to Calliope Judkin

Freebie for you—your man is on the move. He's
looking all suspicious, too, acting like he's afraid
someone's watching him (as if). Don't say I never did
anything for you.

"I think it's safe to say we've got the real bird,"
Calliope said, after reading over the letter from Alphonse
Marchetti.

"Duh," said Bud, watching as Misti read the other

papers. Her eyebrows were shooting up as she read and her eyes kept widening. "What does that stuff say, Misti?"

"Oh, man, you guys." Misti's eyes shone. "This is going to be so awesome. Check it out. I mean, if I do it right."

Calliope frowned. "Do what right?"

"Watch. Just watch." Misti leaned over the bird and then, really casually, tapped it on the head three times, followed by two taps to the tail. Then she counted to three and tapped the head again once.

Nothing happened.

"Yeah, that was great," Calliope said. "So anyway . . ."

"No, wait! Wait, just hold on." Misti consulted the papers and leaned over the bird again, lightly tapping the head three times and the tail twice. "One one thousand, two one thousand, three one thousand," she counted carefully, and then tapped the head again.

The Marchetti Bird fluttered its head and then tucked it under one wing.

"Oh, man, this *ROCKS*!" Misti said, jumping up and bouncing in a circle. "You know what this is? These are the instructions telling how you get the bird to do all of its stuff!"

Calliope looked doubtful. "I don't recall reading anything about Marchetti bopping his bird on the head."

Misti shook her head. "No, I'm just doing that because I'm lame and don't have it down. According to this, when you know the timing of the sequences, you barely have to touch the bird. So it would just look like I was swirling my hands around her in a magicky way."

"That's pretty awesome, Misti," Laurie said, watching her jealously. Misti was controlling the Marchetti Bird. How cool was that?

But the bad feeling in her stomach wasn't going away. Laurie cleared her throat. "I don't see how this is going to work, though, do you?"

"What do you mean?" Bud said, watching as Misti concentrated on the papers again. As soon as she put them down, he was totally going to try that tapping thing.

Laurie frowned. "What do we do? We've got evidence now. Do we just call Principal Winkle and tell him about all this stuff?"

"Well, it's proof, isn't it?" Bud said. Misti didn't look like she was planning to put down those papers anytime soon.

"Yeah, but I just don't know how seriously they'll

take it if it's just handed to them by a bunch of kids."

Bud bit his lip. She had a point. When he and Laurie had found the treasure at the beginning of the school year, it had been great, but it had been a bone of contention for some of the staff at the school. Betty Abernathy, for one.

"Well, sure they will," Bud said doubtfully. "They'll have to take it seriously."

"But do you think they'll make the connection? Between LeFranco's dad in the picture and what's happening now? Because it's pretty obvious to me that LeFranco's dad was one of Bull Stratton's bruisers, and what LeFranco's doing now is all connected." Laurie pointed at the picture on the coffee table.

"Yeah, I think you're right." It was clear to him anyway, from the papers in the bird.

"But can you picture a bunch of kids saying, 'Hey, Mr. Big-Time News Editor-in-Chief, your dad was involved in organized crime'? I mean, that's the *MOB*." Laurie shrugged and flopped back in the chair melodramatically. "Oh, what difference does it make? Even if they do make the connections, they'll push us to the side anyway. It'll be all over for us. No more secret room. No more bird."

"No!" Misti said, grabbing the bird. "We can't tell them, then! Not yet, okay?"

"But if we don't tell them, they'll shut down the school!" Laurie didn't want to hand over the bird and the room, but what choice did they have? The bird was the key to everything.

Calliope stood up. "That's why we should take it to my friend at the newspaper. He'll control the story, which means *we'll* control it. Plus we'll take LeFranco down for sure!" Calliope squatted next to Misti and the Marchetti Bird. "We've got the real bird! They'll know it's true!"

"No! That's why we don't say a thing until we've figured out what to do. Because once we tell, there's no going back. I just wish we could take down LeFranco and save the school without losing everything else." Laurie sighed. She wanted to make sure they were doing the right thing. But no matter what they did, they were going to be losing something.

What We Need to Prove
by Laurie Madison, rising seventh grader
1. That LeFranco is lying about the bird.
   (Evidence, we have real bird—check.)

2. That Maria Tutweiler is innocent. (Evidence, letter from Marchetti—check.)

3. That LeFranco has a generations-old vendetta. (Evidence, photo—check.)

Pros and Cons of Proving It

PROS:

1. Clear Maria Tutweiler's name, save school. (AGAIN, addendum by Bud Wallace.)

2. Fame, fortune, etc. (Which is not all it's cracked up to be, addendum by Laurie Madison.) (But is still pretty great, addendum by Calliope Judkin.)

3. LeFranco goes down.

CONS:

1. Have to give up secret room.

2. Have to give up bird. (Addendum by Misti Pinkerton.)

"What we need to do is vote," Laurie said finally. They'd gone over the same points over and over again until she felt sick of the whole thing. "We need to be fair and diplomatic about this."

"Right." Bud nodded. "Okay, everyone in favor of telling about the room to bring down LeFranco, raise your hand." He looked around. Everyone's hand was raised. "Okay, now everyone in favor of keeping it secret, raise your hand." Since they'd all voted for telling, there wasn't much point in holding the second vote, but Bud believed in being thorough.

One hand shot up. Bud rolled his eyes. "Misti, you can't raise your hand for both, okay?"

"But that's how I feel!" Misti whispered. "I want to vote for both."

"Can I change my vote to both? I vote for both too," Laurie said. Sure, she was sabotaging her own vote, but she couldn't help it.

"NO! No voting for both!" Bud said, although he secretly felt like voting for both options himself. This was hopeless. They weren't getting anywhere. "We'll try again. Everyone who votes for—"

Suddenly Misti grabbed his arm. "Shh," Misti whispered. "Hallway!"

"LeFranco?" Bud said, hurrying to the door in the corner and listening intently.

"Sounds like it," Laurie whispered, silently tiptoeing over.

She opened the door carefully and crept out into the passageway, past the library and on to the second screen, where they'd seen LeFranco's secret meeting before.

It was him.

She could see him with Reginald, and it looked like they were arguing about something. Or at least that's how it looked to Laurie. People don't usually poke each other in the chest in casual conversations, but maybe LeFranco was just different that way.

"Montana said he was on the move," Calliope whispered. "What are they talking about?"

"I don't know," Bud whispered. "We can't hear." He shot her his patented shut-up look. It seemed to work. Calliope jostled for a good position in front of the screen, but she kept her mouth shut.

LeFranco was still poking Reginald in the chest and talking angrily in a low voice. "'I *can't*' is not an option, Reginald. '*I can't*' doesn't help me. Now you figure out a way to make this bird sing, or you'll wish you'd never heard of the Marchetti Bird. And don't even *think* about telling me *you can't*."

Reginald looked upset. "Look, I've done what you asked. But this bird won't do anything it wasn't designed to do. And this bird wasn't supposed to sing."

"Then you come up with a reason why it won't. No one knows how the Marchetti Bird worked, Reginald.

Be creative. Find a broken key or something, some reason it's broken. But make it believable. I'll give you twenty-four hours. I'm scheduling another press conference, and this bird had better perform or have a decent reason for not performing."

"A key, sure." Reginald nodded, rubbing at his chest. Laurie felt sure he was going to have a bruise. "I can do that."

"See that you do," LeFranco sneered. "And give my regards to Eunice and Rosalie." Without another word, he turned and stormed out of the school.

Reginald stood for a moment just staring at the floor. Then he wiped his hand over his face, took out his rag, and started polishing a plaque on the wall. Laurie turned away from the screen. She couldn't bear to see the look on his face.

"See, I knew that singing stuff would put LeFranco on the run. Ha!" Calliope whispered. "We've got him!" Then she turned and hurried back to the room.

"Who are Eunice and Rosalie?" Misti whispered when Calliope was gone.

Laurie shook her head.

Bud looked at Laurie and Misti. "We have to tell, don't we?"

Laurie nodded. They had to stop LeFranco, one way or another. Reginald didn't deserve to be treated that way. She didn't know what LeFranco had on him, but it had to stop. "You're right. We don't have a choice."

~

"So how do we do it?" Bud said solemnly. Now that they'd officially decided to give up the room, it was easier to accept and make real plans.

"Maybe do something with the scavenger hunt? We could pretend we were setting up the hunt and lead them here," Laurie said. "Then they'd see for themselves. If we play it right, they won't even know that we'd found it all before."

Bud nodded. "That's good. We could totally do that. We've got that meeting with Miss Abernathy and Principal Winkle anyway," he said, writing it down on his notepad.

"We need to figure out what LeFranco has on Reginald, too," Calliope said.

"Add it to the list," Misti said, practicing making the Marchetti Bird's wings flap. She was getting pretty good. The tapping was much less obvious.

"Can I try?" Bud sidled over to the bird. "What do I do?"

"Just tap tap tap on the butt, pet pet on the wings, and then wait five seconds and tap the nose," Misti explained. "She's a good bird," she said gloomily.

Bud tapped, petted, and then counted to five and tapped again. Nothing happened. "Did I do it wrong?"

Misti shook her head. "You did fine. She's just temperamental."

Laurie tried to smile. She hated to see Misti lose that bird. Sure, it was just a big piece of metal, but the two seemed to have bonded, somehow. And waiting was only going to make it worse. "Right. Well. We know what we have to do. You know what? Forget about waiting for the scavenger hunt. Let's do it now." She just wanted to get it over with. If she thought for too long about what they were giving up, she'd change her mind.

"Right." Bud stood up. "Let's go. Then it'll all be over."

Misti kissed the Marchetti Bird on the head and carefully placed it on the coffee table, in prime position to be seen from the door. Then she picked up her book bag and helped pull Calliope to her feet. The others had just gathered their things when a creak from the corner of the room made them freeze.

The passageway door in the corner was opening.

"The ghost!" Misti squealed.

"Run!" Bud croaked.

"YOU!" Laurie said as a figure emerged from the secret passageway. Laurie blinked hard. She couldn't believe what she was seeing. It just didn't seem possible.

"Oh, I'm sorry, dear, I thought you had all gone home." Miss Lucille patted her old-lady hair and tucked her feather duster under her arm. "No hurry, I can come back later." She turned and started back through the secret passage.

"NO!" Laurie said, rushing forward and clutching Miss Lucille's arm. "Wait!"

Miss Lucille took a step back, like Laurie had suddenly turned into a rabid wolverine. But it was still Miss Lucille, so like a rabid wolverine that needed comforting. "It's okay, I'm right here, dear." She patted Laurie on the hand with a worried expression on her face.

"You know?" Misti said, her face blank with shock. "You know about the room?"

"You knew about us?" Bud said. And here he thought they'd been so secret. "How did you know?"

"There goes my exclusive," Calliope muttered, flopping down on the couch.

Miss Lucille gave them a worried smile. "Well, of course I knew. I've known about this room since I was a young girl. Maria Tutweiler shared the secret with me herself. And as for you, Bud," she said, eyes twinkling, "someone has a bad habit of leaving the lights on when they leave."

"Oh, man," Bud groaned. He hadn't even thought about turning out the lights. His dad had always said that his sloppiness would get him into trouble one day. He just hadn't figured on that day being so soon.

"But how did you come in?" Laurie said, looking at the open door. "There's another way in?"

Miss Lucille laughed. "Oh, yes, I prefer to use my private entrance. I assume you've been using the outdoor entrance?"

Laurie nodded. "We kind of messed it up, though." She hated to think of what Miss Lucille was going to say when she saw that shed floor.

"It was already in quite a state," Miss Lucille said, waving her hand dismissively. "Until you started using it, I hadn't realized it was still functional."

"Other entrances? Now you tell us," Bud grumbled.

"When we were in the library the other day, why didn't you tell us you knew?" Laurie asked. Things would've been so much easier if they'd realized she knew.

Miss Lucille looked at Laurie with a strange expression on her face. "You didn't ask."

Typical, Bud thought as he sat down on the footstool. "Yeah, well, it doesn't matter now, since we have to tell everybody about the room anyway."

"Tell who about the room?" Miss Lucille unfurled her feather duster and started dusting. "Why would you tell anyone about it?"

Bud caught himself before he rolled his eyes at Miss Lucille. But really, talk about obvious. "Principal Winkle and the rest of them. If we tell, we can save the school and bring down LeFranco."

Miss Lucille blinked at Bud but didn't say anything.

He decided to try again. "See, once they see the room and the bird, they'll know the truth. Maria Tutweiler wasn't a murderer. There are papers there that prove it. We found them."

"So she didn't murder Marchetti the Magician?" Miss Lucille clasped her hands together. "Well, that is good news! I'm sure you're pleased."

"Uh, yeah," Laurie said. Pretty much understatement of the year, but yeah. A little disturbing that Miss Lucille wasn't counting herself in the "pleased" group, but whatever.

"I told you Maria Tutweiler would never do a silly thing like leave the Marchetti Bird on a storage shelf. Why, she's been safe and sound here with me this whole time." She tickled the top of the Marchetti Bird's head with her feather duster.

"Yeah. Well, good job," Laurie said.

"But you've forgotten something very important about Maria Tutweiler," Miss Lucille said, carefully putting the feather duster on the desk. "Maria Tutweiler was very fond of secrets."

"Uh, yeah," Laurie agreed. Apparently she was going for her Most Inarticulate Student badge.

"I've kept this room secret for decades," Miss Lucille said, rubbing the edge of the desk. "More than half a century."

"Yeah, well, we like keeping it secret too, but we don't have a lot of choice," Bud said helplessly. He looked up at Miss Lucille, and the expression on her face gave him a sudden surge of hope. "Do we?"

Miss Lucille smiled. "The Marchetti Bird isn't the only bit of magic Alphonse Marchetti left in this school. I believe he may have one last trick up his sleeve."

~

Our Plan
by Calliope Judkin, ace reporter
~~Okay, so get this, they're planning to~~
~~They actually want us to~~
~~So they think that we can~~
Forget it, it's just too stupid to write down.
We're going to get caught for sure.

Our Plan
by Bud Wallace, rising seventh grader
~~Okay, so what we'll do is~~
~~So what we were thinking was~~
~~First, we get together and~~
Forget it, it's just too awesome to write down.
It's going to work for sure.

‣PART EIGHT‣

SHOWTIME

EMAIL

FROM: BUD WALLACE

TO: PRINCIPAL MARTIN WINKLE, BETTY ABERNATHY, AND
    OLIVIA HUTCHINS

CC: LAURIE MADISON

SUBJECT: Scavenger Hunt

Hi,

I just wanted to write and let you know how
much Laurie and I are looking forward to the
scavenger hunt meeting tomorrow. I think you'll
be very excited by what we have to tell you.

Yours,

Bud Wallace

EMAIL

FROM: PRINCIPAL MARTIN WINKLE

TO: BUD WALLACE AND LAURIE MADISON

CC: BETTY ABERNATHY, OLIVIA HUTCHINS

SUBJECT: Scavenger Hunt

Thank you, Bud. We'll have a lot to discuss.

Your Princi"PAL",

Martin Winkle

EMAIL

FROM: CALLIOPE JUDKIN

TO: RON BECKER, REPORTER, *DAILY HERALD*

SUBJECT: Tomorrow

Hi, Ron,

I can't give you specifics, but let's just say it
would be in your best interest to be at the school
tomorrow. There's a scavenger hunt meeting. I
can say no more.

Calliope

EMAIL

FROM: RON BECKER, REPORTER, *DAILY HERALD*

TO: CALLIOPE JUDKIN

SUBJECT: Very Funny

What's up, Calliope?

Ron

EMAIL

FROM: CALLIOPE JUDKIN

TO: RON BECKER, REPORTER, *DAILY HERALD*

SUBJECT: Trust me.

You'll thank me. Also, here's a tip. Look into
the relationship between Reginald Moore and

Walker LeFranco. I think you'll find an interesting
connection there.

Calliope

WHILE YOU WERE OUT

FOR *Police Chief Skip Burkiss*

Skip,

You got an anonymous tip. Something about
some scavenger hunt at Tuckernuck Hall?
Sounds like it's unrelated to the protests
they've been talking about, but they were
very insistent that you check it out. I told
them you'd be there.

Also, don't forget I'm taking a half day
tomorrow.

Luralene

Note left in Reginald Moore's school mailbox

Reginald,
I need to change our meeting place
tomorrow. Meet me outside the library
instead.

See you soon,
LeFranco

Note left on Walker LeFranco's car outside his house

LeFranco,
I need to change our meeting place
tomorrow. Meet me outside the library
instead.
See you soon,
Reginald

"I still think his windshield was a weird place to leave it. Do you really think LeFranco's going to buy that?" Bud said nervously. Now that they were actually putting their plan into action, he was a lot less confident about it. If this blew up, it had the potential to blow up massively. Forging notes to LeFranco and Reginald was one thing, but Calliope had even called the police chief. That sure didn't seem like a great idea now.

"Where else was I supposed to leave it? The only other option was for me to hack into Reginald's and LeFranco's emails, and I'm sorry, but there are just some things I'm not capable of, okay?" Calliope was definitely on edge too.

"Okay, fine! It just doesn't scream Reginald to me, that's all."

"Can it, you guys," Laurie interrupted. "We don't need this right now. We've got to meet with Winkle in what, ten minutes? Where's Misti?"

Bud glanced at his watch. "She's late. Shoot. We can't do this without her."

"She'll be here," Laurie said, eyeing the door. At least she'd better be. Without Misti, they didn't have a plan at all.

How to Explain Being Late
by Misti Pinkerton

1. Explain about meeting the secret "friend," even though it'll weird them out right before the plan. (Verdict: NO.)
2. Old standby—bedazzling accident. (Verdict: YES.)

"Sorry, guys, bedazzling accident. You understand," Misti said as she rushed into the secret room. She just hoped that nobody would notice her complete lack of bedazzled accessories. Laurie gave her a weird look, but thankfully, no one seemed to notice anything was up.

"No problem. Did you bring it?" Laurie looked at the bag in Misti's hand.

"Got it." Misti held up the bag. "The toy microphone's right here, complete with fresh batteries. I've got it on the echo setting. I think we're all set. Everything in place?"

"Yep." Bud took a deep breath. "So we all know what to do?"

Laurie and Misti nodded. Calliope shrugged.

"Good," Bud said. "Laurie? It's showtime."

—⟋—

EMAIL

FROM: PRINCIPAL MARTIN WINKLE

TO: BETTY ABERNATHY

SUBJECT: Meeting today

Betty,

Let me do the talking in the meeting today, why don't we? These kids are going to be devastated about the scavenger hunt being canceled—you saw Bud Wallace's email. I'm going to do my best to break it to them gently.

Best,

Marty

EMAIL

FROM: BETTY ABERNATHY

TO: PRINCIPAL MARTIN WINKLE

SUBJECT: You're the principal.

You'll handle it the way you want. Just remember, it hurts less when the Band-Aid is pulled off quickly.

Betty

———

"Kids, we need to talk about the scavenger hunt." Principal Winkle ushered Laurie and Bud inside his office and directed them to the seats in front of his desk. Betty Abernathy was perched on a tall stool next to the desk. He wished she didn't look so smug about the whole thing. If he didn't know better, he'd think she was happy about what he was about to do. "Mrs. Hutchins isn't here yet, but I think we can go ahead and start without her."

Bud smiled up at Principal Winkle as he sat down. "I think you're really going to like what we've done. See, we've got it all worked out—"

"Kids," Principal Winkle interrupted. "I'm afraid we're going to shut the scavenger hunt down." Principal Winkle tried not to make eye contact as he sat down at his desk. He didn't want to see their little crushed faces.

He'd seen Bud and Laurie around the school every day—he knew how hard they'd been working on this.

Bud and Laurie both just stared at him blankly. This was not part of the plan.

"Shut down?" Laurie finally said. "But. No." She shot a desperate look at Bud. "You can't shut us down!"

"You heard Principal Winkle, Laurie," Betty Abernathy said, suppressing a smirk. "His word is final."

"No, you don't understand, you *CAN'T*!" Bud said, glaring at her. He wouldn't be surprised if she was the one behind the whole shutting-down thing. She'd been crabby about the scavenger hunt ever since the first day, when they'd asked about using a jigsaw to make a hole in the cafeteria wall.

"I'm sorry, kids, but this game just isn't appropriate in light of recent media events," Principal Winkle said slowly. This was turning out to be worse than he'd thought. "I'm not canceling it completely. We're just putting it on hold for the time being."

"No," Bud said, jumping to his feet. He shot Laurie a wild-eyed look. "Principal Winkle, you don't understand. You really don't. We've already put the clues out. It's all set up. You just have to look at them, okay? Just once."

"Bud, I'm sorry—" Principal Winkle started.

"Please!" Laurie said. "Shut it down afterward, that's fine, but you just have to look at it once? Please?"

Laurie tried to fight the panic rising in her chest. They'd made allowances for things going wrong. They knew their plan wasn't foolproof. But they had figured they'd at least be allowed to try.

"Don't be ridiculous," Betty Abernathy said. "There's no room for discussion. Good-bye, children."

"But Principal Winkle—" Laurie begged.

"Have some respect, Miss Madison. Now run along, both of you." Betty Abernathy gave them a pinched smile.

Laurie felt a bony hand clamp down on her shoulder and turned in time to see Miss Abernathy clamp her other hand down on Bud's shoulder. She shot him a desperate look as Miss Abernathy propelled the two of them toward the office door.

Just as she was about to physically push them out, Olivia Hutchins rushed in.

"I'm so sorry to be late, guys! You wouldn't believe the traffic. I think it's those protests they were talking about. People are everywhere." She put her bag down and then looked around in confusion. "I'm not that late, am I? Did I miss it?"

"Please, Mrs. Hutchins. We've got the hunt all set up. Please, just see what we've done," Laurie pleaded.

"Miss Abernathy and I were just telling the kids that we're putting the scavenger hunt on hold. It's just not the time for it." Principal Winkle looked apologetic.

"Okay," Mrs. Hutchins said. "That makes sense."

She looked at Bud and Laurie for a long minute, and then shifted her gaze to rest on Betty Abernathy. She gave Betty a tight-lipped smile. "But that doesn't mean we can't go ahead and see what they've got set up, does it?" She turned to Principal Winkle. "If it's all set up . . ."

"It is!" Bud said, brightening. "Promise!"

Principal Winkle looked at Bud and Laurie. He deliberately didn't look at Betty Abernathy. He sighed. "I don't see what it would hurt. If it's all set up."

"Great!" Bud and Laurie exchanged grins and discreetly low-fived each other. They were back on track.

EMAIL
FROM: POLICE CHIEF SKIP BURKISS
TO: LURALENE CLATTERBUCK
Luralene,
I'm at the school. There doesn't seem to be

anything going on. This scavenger hunt thing—is
it some kind of joke of yours?
I'm not laughing.
Skip

Out of office automatic message from Luralene Clatterbuck

I will be out of the office for the rest of the day.
If you need immediate assistance, contact Police
Chief Skip Burkiss. If this is you, Skip, I told you I
was taking the day. Ask me tomorrow.
Luralene

Bud had just pulled the first clue out of his pocket
when Police Chief Skip Burkiss strolled up and tapped
Principal Winkle on the shoulder.

Principal Winkle blanched. "Chief! Um. How can I
help you?"

Skip Burkiss tipped his hat to Principal Winkle and
chewed on a toothpick. "Just here to observe. Got a tip
about the scavenger hunt."

Betty Abernathy shot a furious look at Laurie and Bud.

"Not me," said Laurie, holding up her hand like she
was under oath.

"Me either," said Bud. He was really glad Calliope had taken care of that part of the plan. He would've hated to lie.

"Excellent, excellent," Principal Winkle said, bobbing up on the balls of his feet. "We were just getting started." Sweat was beginning to pop up along his hairline. A police investigation was the last thing he needed. The only thing that would make it worse was having the press involved.

"Sorry I'm late." Ron Becker ran up, his camera swinging from the strap around his neck. "Has it started?"

Principal Winkle stared at him blankly. "Started?"

Police Chief Burkiss shifted his toothpick to the other side of his mouth.

"For the scavenger hunt? Reporter Ron Becker for the *Daily Herald*. I got a tip." Ron Becker pulled a small notebook out of his pocket.

"Uh. No, we were just starting," said Principal Winkle, shooting Bud and Laurie a black look.

They blinked back innocently. Halos were practically forming over their heads.

Bud cleared his throat and looked down at the clue. "Okay, so the first clue. These are all kind of rough still, since we were mainly focused on figuring out the locations. But you'll get the gist."

Rough was an understatement. They'd figured out the clues on the back of a paper bag while Calliope stuck the note onto LeFranco's windshield. That clue would've needed a lot more work to qualify as rough.

Bud glanced nervously at Laurie and started reading. "*Tuckernuckers, brave and true! Today you begin the next phase of the Tuckernuck challenge! You will face hardships on this path, but be stalwart and let neither snow nor rain nor heat nor gloom of night keep you from the treasure. Cluck cluck!*"

Bud lowered the paper. "Stalwart" had been his idea. They'd tried to make the clue sound like the ones Maria Tutweiler had written, and he thought they'd come pretty close. Misti had come up with the cluck cluck part at the end. He wasn't sure that worked, but it was probably fine.

"That's the first clue?" Principal Winkle stared at him.

"That's it," Laurie said. "See, it's like Maria Tutweiler's first one. We didn't want it to be too obvious."

Betty Abernathy harrumphed. "That's ridiculous. How is that a clue?" She looked at Principal Winkle and

Mrs. Hutchins. "Am I wrong?"

Mrs. Hutchins smiled. "I think I understood it. I believe we should go to the mailboxes now?"

Laurie grinned at her. "Let's see." She'd had to look up that post office motto to get it right, but she was glad Mrs. Hutchins had figured it out. When they were writing the clues, it was hard to tell whether they were too hard or too easy. And there was no way they were going with Misti's suggestion. She'd wanted the clue to say "o-gay to the ailbox-may."

The pack of scavenger hunters hurried over to the mailboxes next to the office. A Post-it note was stuck to the top row with completely nondamaging adhesive. Betty Abernathy ripped it off and looked at it disapprovingly. "I believe this is the second clue?" She sniffed.

Bud and Laurie nodded. "Read it," Laurie said.

Betty Abernathy pulled the glasses from the chain around her neck and perched them on her nose. "Ouch!" she said, and frowned. "That's the first word—ouch." She continued reading.

"One hundred pricks I feel without complaint.
Messages I am happy to convey.
Tiny red-capped swords won't make me faint.
I'll tell you how to join the fray."

Mrs. Hutchins tried not to cringe. Bad poetry always made her nauseous.

"It's a poem," Bud said.

"It's a bad poem," Laurie added.

"It's a terrible poem." Mrs. Hutchins suppressed a smile.

"I understand this one, though," Betty Abernathy said, smirking. "I believe it was my idea."

She turned and abruptly trotted away from the mailboxes and down the hall. Laurie and Bud had to jog to keep up with her, but they caught up right outside the bulletin board outside the cafeteria.

Betty Abernathy looked approvingly at the next note, stabbed to the bulletin board with a red pushpin. "Nice."

"You said the bulletin board would be a good place," Laurie said. She still thought the bulletin board idea was

the lamest ever, but they'd figured a little sucking up would do them a world of good. Apparently they'd been right. Betty Abernathy seemed to have thawed out by at least fifteen degrees. Which still didn't put her above freezing, but was a lot better.

Principal Winkle nodded and unpinned the note. "We can work on the poem," he said. And by "work on," he really meant "come up with an entirely different clue." There were just some things that were too painful to bear, and bad poetry was one of them.

Chief Burkiss ambled up, with Ron Becker close behind him, catching up to the rest of the group. They hadn't seen any need to rush. They both looked doubtful and more than a little irritated.

Laurie wasn't surprised. If she'd been given a hot tip and gotten a lousy poem instead, she'd be pretty irritated too. She just hoped they stuck around for the payoff.

Principal Winkle cleared his throat and held the clue up in front of him. "Rabbi Icy Antler." He looked around expectantly.

"Pardon?" Police Chief Skip Burkiss took the toothpick out of his mouth.

Principal Winkle turned red. "I'm sorry, did I say that wrong?" He looked at the paper closely. "Rabbi . . .

Icy Antler. No, that's right."

"I hardly think religious references are appropriate."
Miss Abernathy frowned at Laurie and Bud.

"It's not—" Bud started, but Laurie elbowed him
subtly in the side.

"Let them figure it out!" she hissed. She really wished
they'd hurry up, though. Waiting for them to figure out
the stupid clues was agony, and it wasn't like they were
even particularly involved clues. Maybe they should've
gone with Misti's Pig Latin after all.

Ron Becker raised his pencil like he was in class. "I'm
not familiar with any Rabbi Icy Antler. Is this an indi-
vidual, do you think?"

"Or a nickname," Olivia Hutchins piped up. She
didn't want to think about which staff member might be
nicknamed Rabbi Icy Antler. If she had to guess, she'd
put her money on Betty Abernathy, though.

"Word jumble," Skip Burkiss said, putting his toothpick back in his mouth.

"That's it! It's a word jumble!" Olivia Hutchins said,
clapping her hands together. She was so relieved the kids
didn't call her Rabbi Icy Antler.

The adults all crowded around the piece of paper. "So
we've got two Bs, an I . . . no, two Is, and . . ." Principal

Winkle sighed. "Or you could just tell us what it spells?"
Principal Winkle looked at Laurie and Bud desperately.

Laurie and Bud looked at each other, and Bud nodded slightly.

"Library cabinet," Laurie said finally.

"Cheater," Betty Abernathy muttered under her breath, turning and hurrying off down the hallway toward the library.

Bud grabbed Laurie's arm as the others followed her. "You think Misti's ready?"

Laurie nodded. "She has to be."

**List of Things That Could Go Wrong
by Laurie Madison, rising seventh grader**
1. Everything.
2. See number one.

Miss Lucille was arranging tiny pieces of vegetables on two little dollhouse plates when they arrived. She looked up in surprise. "Can I help you?"

Laurie eyed the plates doubtfully. She had to hand it to Miss Lucille—she was one good actor. She sure seemed surprised to see them, even though she knew they were coming. But that vegetable thing just seemed weird. That was one hundred percent Miss Lucille. It hadn't been in the plan.

Principal Winkle was also eyeing the plates, but he didn't say anything. "May we please see your cabinet?"

Miss Lucille wiped her hands on a cloth and stood up. "Of course! Ponch and Jon can wait a few minutes more for their lunch."

Ponch and Jon clenched their fists and gnawed angrily on the water-bottle holder in their cage. Laurie could tell what they were really hoping to get for lunch. Flesh dripping with blood, and lots of it.

She shuddered and turned away.

Miss Lucille led the group through the library toward her office. It was a small room tucked away in the corner of the library. Laurie tried to breathe normally. On the other side of that wall was the secret passageway, and with the exception of Bud and Miss Lucille, no one had the slightest idea.

Miss Lucille stood next to a large, black wooden cabinet pushed against the back wall of the office. "Not much to see, I'm afraid."

Principal Winkle nodded. "We'll just take a look inside." He opened the cabinet door.

The cabinet was completely empty. The only thing

inside was a small Post-it note stuck to the back wall.

Principal Winkle pulled it out and raised it above his head so everyone could see it, and smiling, he shut the cabinet door. "The next clue!" He walked back out of the room and into the main part of the library.

"Shall we?" He peered down at the clue. "*I am not what I appear to be. But what I reveal will lead you to . . .*" Principal Winkle tapered off and cocked his head to the side. He could almost catch a faint sound coming from nearby.

"Do you . . . hear that?" he said softly, looking up.

"Hear what?" Betty Abernathy snapped.

"Shh," Principal Winkle said, not moving.

"Oh." Mrs. Hutchins sighed, her head up as she caught the faint strains of sound too.

As they stood there, the whole room slowly filled with the song of the Marchetti Bird. No one moved until the last traces of the music had tapered off and disappeared completely.

"That was beautiful," Mrs. Hutchins said, releasing her breath. She hadn't even realized she'd been holding it. "What was that?"

"When the true heir of Alphonse Marchetti is revealed, the Marchetti Bird will sing again." Miss Lucille stood staring off into space, her voice loud and booming in the room.

"Um. What?" Principal Winkle looked at his school librarian nervously. He didn't know any exorcists, and he was afraid he might need one.

Miss Lucille smiled at him. "It's the legend. The Marchetti Bird will reappear when the true heir of Alphonse Marchetti is revealed."

"Oh. Okay." Principal Winkle smiled back weakly. "Learn something new every day."

> NOTE TO SELF
> BY PRINCIPAL MARTIN WINKLE
> 1. CONTACT FATHER GEORGE DOWN AT
>   THE CHURCH, SEE ABOUT RATES FOR
>   EXORCISMS.

"Was that . . ." Mrs. Hutchins hesitated. "Was that the Marchetti Bird?"

Miss Lucille wiped off the countertop casually. "What else could it be?"

> NOTE TO SELF, ADDENDUM
> BY PRINCIPAL MARTIN WINKLE

> 1. CONTACT FATHER GEORGE DOWN AT
>   THE CHURCH, SEE ABOUT RATES FOR
>   EXORCISMS.
> 2. SEE IF THERE ARE GROUP DISCOUNTS.

Miss Abernathy snorted. "Please. Even if Walker LeFranco has found the Marchetti Bird, it would hardly be singing in our library."

"*Follow.*" A soft voice echoed through the library.

Miss Abernathy froze. "What was that?"

"*Follow.*" The voice came again. Laurie could hardly hear it, but it was deep and low and filled the whole room.

Police Chief Skip Burkiss stepped forward, one hand on his holster. "All right now, who said that? Come on out now."

"*Follow the song,*" the voice said, drawing out the words so they flowed into one another.

Laurie shivered. It was really creepy. She exchanged a glance with Bud. He looked as freaked out as she felt, but he gave her a discreet thumbs-up. Misti's microphone was working.

"Who's doing that?" Betty Abernathy looked around wildly. "You think you're clever, kids? This isn't funny."

"It's not us!" Laurie said.

"FOLLOW THE SONG," the voice came again, louder this time.

"We'll follow the song, Alphonse," Miss Lucille said, beaming into the distance.

"Oh, please. Alphonse?" Betty Abernathy's voice was thin, though, and the blood had drained from her face.

"Are we saying this is the voice of Alphonse Marchetti?" Ron Becker scribbled furiously on his notepad.

"We're not saying anything," Principal Winkle said, looking nervously at Becker. "That is not the official opinion of Tuckernuck Hall."

"FOLLOW," the voice said again, more loudly this time.

"We'll follow the song!" Mrs. Hutchins yelled. Then she shrugged at Principal Winkle. "What?"

"Olivia, I—" Principal Winkle started, but his voice was drowned out as the singing started again.

"Quick, follow it!" Mrs. Hutchins took a few tentative steps toward the back wall of the library. "Where is it coming from?"

"It sounds like . . . this direction?" Principal Winkle walked slowly back the way they'd come.

Betty Abernathy cocked her head and then swiveled it to look into the back office. "There." She pointed toward Miss Lucille's office.

The group moved as one mass toward the back office until they reached the door, and then Police Chief Burkiss held out his arm.

"Let me," he said. He slipped his gun out of the holster and slowly entered the office as the others crowded in behind him.

"It . . . it's coming from the cabinet," Principal Winkle said.

"That's impossible." Betty Abernathy said. "We just looked in there. It's empty."

"Well, it is," Principal Winkle said. There was nothing wrong with his ears. At least, he didn't think so.

"Stand back, ma'am." Police Chief Burkiss moved to the side of the cabinet. And as the bird's song died away, in one quick motion he opened the cabinet doors.

There, standing in the center of the cabinet, was the Marchetti Bird.

EMAIL
FROM: PRINCIPAL MARTIN WINKLE
TO: CANDY WINKLE

SUBJECT: Appointment

Sugar Booger, could you remind me to make an appointment with Dr. Simonson? I really need to get my eyes checked.

Kisses,

Your Doodlebug

P.S. I should maybe get my ears checked, too.

Online banner headline on the Daily Herald *website*

MARCHETTI BIRD SINGS!
Online exclusive coming soon.

"That cabinet was empty!" Betty Abernathy rushed forward, but then stopped herself just before she touched the cabinet. She pulled her hands back against her chest and stared at the bird. "There was nothing there."

"Excuse me, ma'am." Police Chief Burkiss stepped forward and quickly inspected the cabinet. Then he gently picked the Marchetti Bird up by the base. Pushing past the others, he carried it out into the library and set it on one of the tables.

"But how did it get there? No one came into the library," Olivia Hutchins said, staring at the bird.

Even Ponch and Jon stopped gnashing their venomous

teeth and stood silently watching the proceedings. The only sound came from Ron Becker's pen as he scribbled on page after page in his notebook.

"Laurie, Bud!" Misti's voice echoed through the hallway as she came barreling into the library. "Did you guys hear that sound?" Misti stopped short. "Oh. Hi, everybody. What's everybody doing?" She blinked innocently.

"We heard it. It was the Marchetti Bird." Laurie pointed at the bird on the table.

"Gosh, that's weird," Misti said, her eyes wide. Laurie cringed. Misti wasn't really an actress. Maybe for silent films she'd be okay, but with her eyes open wide and her mouth in a surprised O, it was like she was playing charades. "Because look who we just found in the hall." Misti turned and pointed dramatically to the doorway as Calliope herded Reginald and LeFranco into the library.

And in Walker LeFranco's hands was the other Marchetti Bird.

EMAIL
FROM: POLICE CHIEF SKIP BURKISS
TO: LURALENE CLATTERBUCK

SUBJECT: Scavenger hunt

Sure hope you're enjoying that day off, Luralene. I've had quite a day myself. You sure do know how to time those half days of yours, don't you?

Skip

"Two birds?" Miss Abernathy said, sitting down carefully on one of the wooden library chairs. She looked like she was about to fall over.

"Now why don't you put that bird you've got there down right next to this one, okay?" Skip Burkiss pointed at the first bird with his toothpick.

"And tell us what you're doing here, while you're at it." Principal Winkle glared at Walker LeFranco. "Or perhaps Reginald can do it?"

Reginald slicked back his hair and shifted uncomfortably. He couldn't seem to take his eyes off the first bird on the table.

Walker LeFranco stepped forward and reluctantly put his bird on the table, next to the other Marchetti Bird.

The difference was amazing. Even though the two birds looked essentially the same, the bird from the cabinet sparkled and seemed to glow in the fluorescent lights. LeFranco's bird looked like he'd gotten it out of a gum machine.

"Is there any law against peddling a false Marchetti Bird, Chief?" Ron Becker said, pencil poised.

Walker LeFranco paled. "There's no evidence it wasn't my bird singing. You have no proof that other bird is real. None. I have proof. Reginald found the real Marchetti Bird."

"Our bird magically appeared in an empty cabinet," Bud said. His voice was maybe a little too gloaty, but Laurie didn't think anybody else noticed.

"Reginald here will swear that mine is real. Won't you, Reginald?" Walker LeFranco said, pushing Reginald forward.

Reginald stared at the floor.

"Walker LeFranco, isn't it true that you hold the leases on the homes of both Reginald Moore's sister and his mother?" Ron Becker waited, his pencil poised over the notebook.

Walker LeFranco shrugged. "I suppose so."

"And did you threaten to evict his family members if he didn't cooperate with your plans?"

LeFranco gave a barky laugh. "That's ridiculous."

Ron Becker nodded and dug around in his briefcase.

"Strange, that's not what I heard when I talked to Rosalie and Eunice Moore. I have their notarized statements right here."

"It's true," Reginald said, rushing over to the police chief. "He tripled their rent, and when they couldn't pay that, he said if I didn't pretend to find the bird, my folks would be out on the streets."

Chief Burkiss nodded and pulled out his handcuffs. "Sounds like blackmail to me. How'd you figure this all out, Becker?"

"I got a tip," Ron Becker said, winking at Calliope.

Headline on Daily Herald *website*

BLACKMAIL CHARGES AGAINST WALKER LEFRANCO
Marchetti Bird evidence faked, school janitor reveals

"What I don't understand, though, is why did the bird sing?" Olivia Hutchins leaned over and looked into the eyes of the real Marchetti Bird. "And where did it come from?"

"The Marchetti Bird will sing when the true heir is

revealed," Miss Lucille said, smiling.

"But what does that mean?" Mrs. Hutchins straightened back up. "What heir?"

"I wonder how this thing works," Bud said, looking closely at the Marchetti Bird. "Gosh, Misti, how do you think it works?"

Laurie rolled her eyes. Those two definitely wouldn't be winning any Academy Awards anytime soon.

Misti went over to the bird, swallowing hard. "I don't know, Bud." Misti sounded like she was reading lines. "Um. But, it's almost . . . um, like you can feel the energy off of it."

She lifted her hands up and waved them over the bird. She had gotten so good, Laurie almost couldn't see her tap the bird on the beak and the head in the proper sequence. She was a natural.

Almost immediately, the bird began to sing.

"Misti Pinkerton is the true heir?" Principal Winkle gasped. He was going to have to revise his impression of the Pinkerton girl. He'd never thought of her as a magician's true successor. It was hard not to think of her in a chicken hat and sequins.

The drawer in the base of the Marchetti Bird slid open, revealing Alphonse Marchetti's letter and the bundle of papers but, strangely, missing the instructions for the Marchetti Bird.

"She's the heir," Miss Lucille said. "The Marchetti Bird has spoken."

Story on the Daily Herald *website*

EXCLUSIVE! Walker LeFranco Faked Evidence to Shut Down Tuckernuck Hall. Real Marchetti Bird reveals truth about Alphonse Marchetti disappearance.

Police Chief Skip Burkiss was leaning against the wall next to the library when Ron Becker hurried into the hallway. Chief Burkiss put his arm out, blocking Becker as he tried to pass.

"Ron." Chief Burkiss smiled. "You got yourself a good story here, don't you now."

Ron nodded.

"And you'll be wanting quotes and whatnot from the police. Especially now that those papers have turned up. Am I right?"

Ron nodded again. He wasn't sure where this was going, but nodding seemed like a good bet.

"That's what I thought." Skip Burkiss straightened up. "Now, I'm not one to tell you your job . . . "

"Of course not, Chief," Ron said. He was itching to get back to the office and post the reports. He'd called in a couple of teaser headlines, but this was big. And he wouldn't put it past LeFranco to post his own confession to drive up sales of the *Morning News*. "Any suggestions, though?"

"Just when you say that the bird was found, saying it was in the library cabinet might be enough. No need to go into all that extra stuff about the singing and the disembodied voices and the bird appearing in an empty cabinet. That's the kind of thing that makes a reporter lose credibility, know what I mean? Especially when it's not backed up by the police."

"Right." Ron nodded. He hadn't been sure how he was going to spin the whole magically appearing bird part anyway. Probably better to leave it out.

"Good, good," Chief Burkiss said, smacking Ron affectionately on the chest. "Now you come to me for any exclusive quotes, you hear?"

Ron nodded, trying not to rub the spot on his chest. He'd have to make a couple of minor changes to his story, but it was no big deal. Nothing too big or noticeable.

From the notebook of Ron Becker

EXCLUSIVE—~~MYSTERIOUS GHOST~~
~~OF ALPHONSE MARCHETTI MAGICALLY~~
~~CONJURES MARCHETTI~~ BIRD, SOLVES
MYSTERY

~~Miraculous~~ Discovery ~~of magical bird,~~
~~guided by disembodied voice of the deceased~~
~~magician and which appeared out of thin air,~~
vindicates founder María Tutweiler.

~~"A voice from beyond the grave led us",~~
~~revealed librarian Miss Lucille.~~

Principal Winkle watched through the window as Ron Becker hurried off down the hallway. "Well, I'm sorry that your scavenger hunt went a little off track," he said. "Maybe we can pick it up later with that . . ." He dug around in his pocket and pulled out the clue. *"I am not what I appear to be. But what I reveal will lead—"*

"It's okay. It was the fake rock out front. That's what that clue's talking about," Laurie blurted out. They'd thought they'd been so clever, writing a clue that hinted about the cabinet. But it wouldn't be too clever to get

Principal Winkle thinking about it too much.

"Oh! Oh, yes, I see. Fake rock. Good idea!" Principal Winkle said, winking. "You know, I have one of those at my house. Genius!"

"Genius!" Laurie echoed. Great. Now if she and Bud ever needed to break into Principal Winkle's house, they'd know just where to look. Laurie sighed. Real smart.

Principal Winkle stood up. "Well, I think we can just leave this for—"

"Sir, excuse me, sir." Candy Winkle's voice rang out through library. They turned in time to see her pushing her way into the library, hot on the tail of the man in the floppy hat and the I HEART MARIA TUTWEILER shirt. "Sir, I'm sorry, but the tours are *canceled*." Candy Winkle threw up her hands. "Marty, explain to him, please? He just won't listen to me."

"I'm sorry. I was running late," the man said, taking his hat off and twisting it in his hands.

"That's okay. Hi, Arnold," Misti said, hurrying over.

"Hi, Misti," the man said, brightening. He turned to Candy Winkle. "I have an appointment with this young lady. I'm not here for a tour."

Candy Winkle rolled her eyes. "That's what he keeps saying, but really."

Misti put her hand on the man's arm. "Guys, this is Arnold Mars. He's with that carnival that's out on Route 3 past the Tastee Freez."

Arnold Mars raised a hand and waved shyly. "Arnold Mars."

"The carnival?" Laurie tried to remember where she'd heard about that carnival recently. "You're the one leaving those messages!" Laurie said accusingly. She didn't care what the guy's name was. He still creeped her out.

"Yeah, which you guys didn't even bother to check on," Misti said. "So I did. And I think you're going to want to hear what he has to say." Misti crossed her arms. "Show them the picture, Arnold."

Arnold Mars reached into his pocket, pulled out an old leather wallet, and took out a faded photo. He held it out to Laurie. "It's the only copy I have. But that's me, and my dad, and my mom, and my little sister."

Laurie took the picture and looked at it skeptically.

Then she gasped. "But that's . . ." She pointed at the photo wildly.

Arnold nodded. "My dad, Big Al Mars."

Laurie handed the picture to Bud. "It's Alphonse Marchetti."

Calliope pulled out her cell phone and dialed. "Ron? You might want to come back here."

TRAFFIC CITATION

For: Ron Becker

Arresting officer: Kirby Bruce

Notes: Subject was seen talking on his cell phone while driving, making an illegal U-turn, and going 75 in a 30-mile-per-hour zone.

Ranted about "true heir."

May be psychologically unstable.

HOLDING FOR FURTHER INVESTIGATION AND/OR TREATMENT.

Phone message for Calliope Judkin

Calliope, your little friend "Ron" called you earlier. He said something about his one phone call? He didn't leave a number.

Your Mother

"My dad didn't like to talk about his past," Arnold Mars

said, taking a doughnut from the box in the middle of the table. Candy Winkle had run to the office for snacks. She hoped it would make up for berating Arnold Mars for the past half hour. She'd been sure he was just a creepy tour fan.

"But he told me that if I ever wanted to know about him, I should just talk to Maria Tutweiler, and she could tell me."

"Wow, that must've been a long time ago," Bud said, eyeing the doughnuts. He wasn't sure if they were for everyone or just for Arnold.

"It was. And I guess I waited too long. That's why I've been on these tours, and why I wanted to talk to you kids. I thought you might know something."

"Sorry we blew you off," Laurie said. "But you should've just said. We thought you were a weirdo."

Arnold laughed, spewing white powder around the table and onto the remaining doughnuts. Bud decided he wasn't hungry after all.

"So are you a magician too?" Misti asked. "Do you perform at the carnival?"

Arnold shook his head and wiped his mouth. "I'm Big Al, of Big Al's Amazing Ice Sculptures. My dad was the real Big Al, and I just kept the name. I didn't even know he could do magic. Weird, huh?"

"Yeah." Laurie nodded. She was glad that Alphonse Marchetti had gone on to have a family and a happy life, though. And you only had to look at the Marchetti Bird to know that he'd been a talented artist. Those ice sculptures probably really were amazing.

"So you're the real heir of Alphonse Marchetti," Misti said mournfully. She'd only been the heir for few moments, but they'd been nice moments.

"I'd say we both are," Arnold said, waving his hand over the Marchetti Bird. It just sat there. "I'm not an heir for the old Alphonse Marchetti. Sounds like he's got two heirs—one heir for each of his lives."

"That sounds nice," Misti said, brightening.

"We'll make sure to take good care of your dad's bird, too," Principal Winkle said. "Betty, make a note—we'll need a new display case for the entry hall. We'll make it the centerpiece of the school."

Police Chief Burkiss cleared his throat from the other side of the room, where he was casually listening. "Seems to me that item is actually the property of that gentleman there."

He tipped his toothpick in Arnold Mars's direction.

Principal Winkle paled. "Yes, I see, but . . ."

"That seems fair," Misti said sadly. "It was his dad's."

Arnold Mars smiled. "That's wonderful. It's really mine?" he said, craning his neck to look at Chief Burkiss.

"Far as I'm concerned."

"Great. Then, Misti, I'd like to give it to you." Arnold waved his hands around the bird again and petted it on the head. "It doesn't speak to me the way it does to you."

"Really?" Misti grabbed Arnold Mars in a huge hug and then beamed at Laurie and Bud. "I'm going to be a magician!"

Draft of a flyer

> Come see the debut of the amazing
> MISTI THE MAGICIAN
> WATCH as she performs amazing
> illusions
> BE AMAZED by the magical
> MARCHETTI BIRD
> This week only—SPECIAL GUEST
> ASSISTANT ARNOLD MARS

"I can't believe Alphonse Marchetti's disappearing cabinet was here all this time," Laurie said to Miss Lucille once the other adults had all left.

"It made a perfect entrance to the secret passageway from the library," Miss Lucille said, feeding Ponch and Jon their lunch. The excitement of the afternoon had been almost too much for them, and they were only able to bare their teeth threateningly once or twice before collapsing back on their nest of cedar chips and the bones of their enemies.

"Was that true, about the legend of the Marchetti Bird?" Misti said, stroking the bird's head. "Did somebody really say that about the true heir?"

"Of course," Miss Lucille said, carefully placing tiny baby corns next to Ponch and Jon.

"Who?"

"Why, me, silly," Miss Lucille said, chuckling. "Little scatterbrain."

"It's too bad we all can't use that cabinet to get to the secret room," Bud said. "Someone's going to get suspicious about the shed eventually."

"Yes, students aren't allowed to use the back office of the library," Miss Lucille said sadly, patting Laurie on the hand. "So it's lucky that you four are now my official library assistants."

"We are?" Laurie wasn't sure that was a good thing.

"And of course library assistants are permitted to use the cabinet as needed."

"Really?" It was definitely a good thing. Laurie didn't even mind the hand rubbing if she could use that disappearing cabinet to get to the secret room. "That's really cool!"

"Yeah, thanks, Miss Lucille," Bud said. He could deal with a little bit of crazy if it meant they could get to the secret room whenever they wanted.

"We'll still have to fix that shed floor somehow so they won't notice, but I've got that all figured out." Laurie grinned.

"Wonderful!" Miss Lucille said, patting Laurie on the cheek. "Now, new assistants, for your first assignment, I'd like you to help Ponch and Jon get settled in their new Popsicle-stick sanctuary."

Bud and Laurie looked at each other in horror. "Ponch and Jon?"

"Of course!" Miss Lucille handed them the elaborate gerbil annex she'd constructed. "After all, they know you two already!"

Ponch and Jon gave the gerbil equivalent of smiles, their teeth dripping with venom.

Headline in the Daily Herald

> # WALKER LEFRANCO PLEADS GUILTY
> # TO BLACKMAIL, FRAUD
> ## *Blames emotional stress*

Sidebar on the Morning News *website*

Editor-in-Chief Walker LeFranco resigns

Our editor-in-chief, Walker LeFranco, has resigned his position as head of the *Morning News*, effective immediately. He cited the emotional stresses of the job and says he plans to spend more time with his family.

EMAIL

FROM: LAURIE MADISON

TO: BUD WALLACE, MISTI PINKERTON, AND CALLIOPE JUDKIN

SUBJECT: Put on your party hats!

To celebrate saving Maria Tutweiler's reputation *and* keeping the secret room, let's all meet tomorrow at fifteen hundred hours for board games, snacks, and fun! Calliope, this is all off the record. See you tomorrow at you know where!

Laurie

P.S. Be warned—Miss Lucille is planning to bring a Jell-O mold.

P.P.S. By fifteen hundred hours I mean three o'clock.

EMAIL

FROM: CALLIOPE JUDKIN

TO: LAURIE MADISON, BUD WALLACE, AND MISTI PINKERTON

SUBJECT: Jell-O WHAT?

Thanks for the heads-up. I'm on it. I have a contact who's a certified Master Snacker (Montana).

Don't worry, Laurie, I'll be discreet. But sometimes you need the advice of a professional.

Calliope

EMAIL

FROM: JANET DAVIS AT THE TUCKERNUCK HALL GIFT SHOP

TO: PRINCIPAL MARTIN WINKLE

SUBJECT: Merch

Principal Winkle,

I think we're going to need to order more

merchandise. We've sold all of the I HEART
MARIA TUTWEILER shirts, and there's a waiting
list ten people long. And that's just this morning.
Thanks,
Janet in the gift shop

EMAIL
FROM: BETTY ABERNATHY
TO: PRINCIPAL MARTIN WINKLE
SUBJECT: Enrollment
Phones have been ringing off the hook with
parents trying to enroll their kids. We aren't
equipped to handle all these students. Also, are
we planning on offering classes in magic? There
seems to be huge demand.
Thanks,
Betty

Note from Horace Wallace, Sr., to Bud Wallace

Hey, kiddo,
I can't help but notice that you're not a big
fan of Flora's foreign film collection. Maybe
this week for movie night you could pick

the movie? I couldn't find any movies about Marchetti, but it looks like there's a good one on Houdini we could check out.
What do you think? I think we have room on the couch if your friends want to come too.
Dad

Note from Bud Wallace to Horace Wallace, Sr.

Thanks, Dad. That Houdini movie sounds awesome. (It doesn't have subtitles, does it?)
Bud

Banner on the Daily Herald *website*

EXCLUSIVE!
Long-lost photo found in Marchetti Bird reveals LeFranco family ties to organized crime, may explain longstanding vendetta against Tuckernuck Hall.

EMAIL
FROM: MRS. WANDA PINKERTON
TO: MR. MEL PINKERTON

SUBJECT: Glitz and Glamour

Mel, on your way home, could you pick me up some more sequins and satin fabric? Probably in a blue. Our Misti's going to be a bedazzling magician!

Thanks,

Wanda

Text message from Calliope Judkin to Montana Judkin

Hey, thanks for your help with the LeFranco case. I've left something for you in your room. Let's call it a bonus.

Text message from Montana Judkin to Calliope Judkin

WOW! Jumbo bag of fun-size Snickers and THREE BAGS OF TWIZZLERS? You ROCK!

Headline on the Daily Herald *website*

EXCLUSIVE: THE MARCHETTI HEIRS, an exclusive interview by our own Calliope Judkin

EMAIL
FROM: CANDY WINKLE
TO: PRINCIPAL MARTIN WINKLE
SUBJECT: The Shed
Snookums,
I took a look at that shed out back, and it's a
lawsuit waiting to happen. That floor looks so
poorly constructed that I think someone could
just fall right through. I think we should hire
contractors to fix it before something happens.
Candy

EMAIL
FROM: PRINCIPAL MARTIN WINKLE
TO: CANDY WINKLE
SUBJECT: Problem Solved
Cupcake,
I've got the shed situation all taken care of.
I've just hired one of our former Cluckers,
Jack Madison, to do some minor repairs at the
school, and he mentioned the shed in particular.
I think you remember him—he's the brother of
Laurie Madison, who's friends with Misti the
Magician?

Kisses,

Your Cuddlebug

EMAIL

FROM: CANDY WINKLE

TO: PRINCIPAL MARTIN WINKLE

SUBJECT: Sorry

Sorry, Sugar, the names Laurie and Misti just aren't ringing a bell with me.

Note from Jack Madison slipped under Laurie Madison's door

Laurie,
You're all set, and your secret is safe with me. And you're right—it was totally worth an afternoon of work to see that room.
That's quite a place you've got there.
Jack

ACKNOWLEDGMENTS

Once again, I have to thank some wonderful people—
Katherine Tegen, Katie Bignell, Steven Malk, and
everyone at Katherine Tegen books.

Big thanks also go out:

To Antonio Caparo, for bringing Laurie, Bud, and
the rest of the gang to life.

To my family, for reading endless versions of the
manuscript.

To Sonya Sones, for taking such great author photos.

To Lois Lowry, for Anastasia Krupnik and for making me love lists, and to Jaclyn Moriarty, for her cool and
inspiring epistolary books.

To Harry Houdini, Thurston the Great Magician,
Harry Kellar, Carter the Great, and other magicians, for
their amazing feats of magic.

And to my parents, for never buying me a BeDazzler.

Discover the first Tuckernuck mystery!

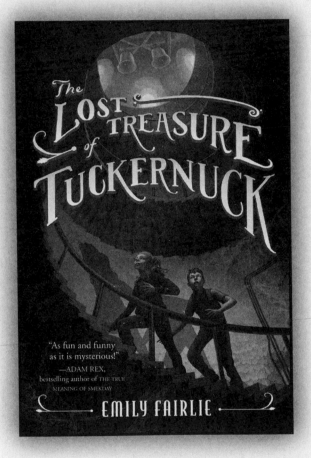

Bud and Laurie set out on a scavenger hunt to solve the eighty-year-old mystery of Tuckernuck Hall!